<u>PRAISE FOR</u> UNHOLY

"Ever since reading *Epiphany*, I have thought J.V. Gachs was a wonderfully talented writer. *Unholy* proves she is also capable of great boldness and intensity. I blushed at the eroticism of this novel but was also taken with the sense of atmosphere, the theme of innocence and 'purity' versus agency and self-actualization, and the way Gachs explores the relationship between pleasure and pain."

-Christi Nogle, Bram Stoker Award® winning author of *Beulah*

"In *Unholy*, the lives of two women bound by destiny and scarred by obligation and suffering intertwine in a brutal and bawdy fight between good and evil. Succumb to JV Gachs' seduction and become a breathless initiate, anointed by blood and desire."

-Angela Sylvaine, author of *Frost Bite* and *Chopping Spree*

"*Unholy* gives readers the glorious lesbian nunsploitation we deserve, complete with a delicious satanic orgy and some genuinely tender moments. Gachs' writing is fun, flirty and a bloody treat."

-Lor Gislason, editor of *Bound in Flesh*

"*Unholy* is a dark, riveting tale of broken people trying to save a broken world amidst the approaching Apocalypse. Sinister, erotic, subversive, and violent, this story will burrow into your soul and stay with you for a long time."

-Pedro Iniguez, author of *Fever Dreams of a Parasite*

"With language rich as pomegranate wine, *Unholy* seduces the reader into a cosmic battle between the divine and the damned."

-Drew Huff, Author of *Free Burn*

"*Unholy* is a seductive novella that makes you question who you have faith in and why. It lets you not just feel, but revel, in what you might think is forbidden. By its final pages, you might just have something (or someone) new to believe in."

-T.T. Madden, author of *The Familialists* and *The Cosmic Color*

"A beautiful, gut-wrenching story of love, loss, and depravity. Gachs paints a deliciously wicked vision of the end of times."

-David-Jack Fletcher, award-winning author of *Raven's Creek*

"Depraved, sensual, and skin crawlingly-creepy, *Unholy* is a bloody horror genre-blender you won't want to miss."

-Chloe Spencer, author of *Mewing* and *An Affinity for Formaldehyde*

"Blood, sex, and the end of the world. J.V. Gach's Unholy is a titillating tale of virginal sacrifice, religious violence, and queer love that will have your heart (and more) pounding from beginning to end."

-A. P. Thayer, author of nightmarist fiction

UNHOLY

J.V. GACHS

MADAXEMEDIA.COM

Paperback ISBN: 979-8-9891730-6-8

eBook ISBN: 979-8-9891730-7-5

This one is for me.

UNHOLY

J.V. GACHS

TWO DAYS

MAGDALENA

“**B**less me, Padre, for I *will* sin,” Sor Magdalena muttered upon sneaking into the chapel in the middle of the night.

The empty, oversized building, a hungry beast, devoured avidly the nun's warmth, and, within seconds, she was freezing. Sor Magdalena crossed her trembling hands under her habit, as if the thin black fabric could protect her from the dread seeping into her bones. *You knew this day would come, come on.* Her teeth, pressed tightly against each other, threatened to break.

The middle-aged nun's steps against the tiles echoed in the large space that would soon be filled with the murmured prayers of the congregation. Sor Magdalena wouldn't join her sisters that morning, nor did she plan to any other morning to come. This was meant to be the last time she ever set foot inside a sacred building. Either she failed and sacred places were no more, or she succeeded and then...

Forget it. It's not the time to think about that.

The sky outside was dark. Leaden. Not even the moonlight bled through the mosaic windows. LED candles on both sides of the aisles contributed to the sorrowful atmosphere. Lacking the dancing golden colors of real fire, the scent of burning wax and incense, the room was but a mere open space smelling of bleach. Aseptic and cold, it was nothing more than an assembly of stones, wood, and nails. It was up to Magdalena to fill the place up with the intensity of her determination. But that wasn't shining so bright.

Sor Magdalena reached the altar and caressed the white cloth's coarse fabric with her fingers, memorizing its texture. How many times had she washed that piece of cloth? That insignificant tablecloth that somehow meant the whole world for her right then. There was nothing special about it other than the fact that it was known. Safe. Holding to it, refusing to leave would spare her life. Seconds turned into eternity while she grasped the cloth. In her head, the clear image of her childhood archangel's multiple eyes contemplated her with disdain. Ashamed, she let go, for the crucifix was her destination.

The wooden image of Jesus Christ stood in front of Sor Magdalena, as it had for most of her life. Half-naked, trapped in an excruciating moan, bleeding over the worn-out tiles. Despite the agony masterfully portrayed by the artist, the image had never looked as empty as it did that night. For the first time since she was a novice, the figure looked just as a piece of carved wood. Lifeless and cold. A mockery of real suffering.

Magdalena approached it, trembling, and she wept, holding the ligneous feet of Christ nailed to the cross. Those doubts, those feelings couldn't be hers. She had been strong, adamant, determined for over thirty years, only to start doubting that night? El Diablo had to be behind it. Tempting her with many more years ahead of her outside the convent's walls. Fear of death wasn't any less painful just because it was the Devil's doing.

"Aparta de mi este cáliz," she whispered, pressing her forehead to the figure's inert feet.

Her tears bathed the wood. Her heart thumped against her habit, fast as a maid's on her first night of love, as a knight's on their last battle. On the verge of becoming both, Magdalena tried for the first time to bargain with her Lord.

"Please…"

The nun hoped the image would move. She daydreamed about his hands under her chin, lifting her head and telling her to stop crying because there was no need. Hoped her devotion would soften his wooden heart and make him stop her. Spare her. How many sleepless nights had she imagined he wouldn't allow her sacrifice for humanity's sake? Wasn't he the shepherd that would leave everything behind to go save that one missing sheep? Wasn't she the most needing human being of them all then? Hadn't he tried to bargain with his Holy Father on his last night on Earth too?

But nothing happened.

Devastated by the Lord's silence in the face of her suffering, she kissed the wood, cleaned her tears, and took a deep breath, ready to retrace her steps towards the doors.

Sor Magdalena shuddered when she looked back at the entrance. A man sat on the last row of benches, his features hidden under a hat, sunglasses, and a thick black jacket. More shadow than flesh, only his pale hands were visible gripping the bench's dark wood.

"He's never once moved for me either," he said in a deep hoarse voice, tinted with a mixture of sorrow and hatred.

"Who are you? What are you doing here? This is a cloistered convent: no one should be here, especially not a man," Sor Magdalena said, although her voice broke, afraid of the answer.

She walked down the aisle towards him.

"A man..." He giggled. "If only I could have chosen to be *a man* like he did," the figure spat the last three words as if they had been rotten food in his mouth.

His nails were bloodied claws sinking into the bench. Splinters dug into his flesh; dark thick blood stained the wood.

Magdalena jumped on the man, grabbing his hat to reveal his features, but there was no one there as soon as she lifted it. She stood terrified, holding the hat in her hand. When she let it fall to the ground, it turned to golden dust.

El Diablo suspected something. Would it ruin her attempts of making an alliance with him, or would he be so proud as to think he had convinced her to turn her heart against Jesus? Wasn't pride what condemned him, after all?

On the threshold, Sor Magdalena removed her headpiece, letting her gray hair fall loose over her shoulders, and gave one last longing look to the unmoved statue of her Lord before she walked out, letting her wimple fall to the ground.

Ana

G iggling couples were Ana's least favorite clients, but today's pair were particularly annoying. When she first opened her sex shop five years ago, she thought this kind of costumer would help her heal. If such a thing was even possible. It had been her therapist's idea, one her whole family backed.

Does one ever heal from having your heart ripped off your chest? Asking for a friend.

"It would keep your mind busy. It would help you stay alive," her sister said one evening, both sharing a cigarette at their mother's kitchen window. "What else would you do with the money?"

"I don't want to think about the money; even watching the numbers on my bank account feels wrong…"

"As a self-employed person, I tell you, there's no faster way to get your day filled and those numbers down than starting your own business." María chuckled, elbowing her sister, trying to get a smile out of her.

There hadn't been many smiles around since Amaya was stolen from them. María seemed to have taken upon herself to cheer everyone.

"I don't know, María, maybe you are right. It must be better than the group," Ana conceded.

From the day her doctor suggested the support group for grieving parents, Ana knew it wouldn't make any difference for her. No one, not even there among the mourners, would really understand the depths of the hole in her chest. Of course, other parents had lost their kids to illness, to negligence, to accidents... Children whose hearts stopped beating inside their mother's wombs. And all of them were devastated. Lost. It wasn't her intention to dismiss their suffering. But it infuriated her because nothing came even close to how Amaya had gone. All Ana got from those meetings was rage. Deep animal rage at the other parents' speeches, and tears, and sympathy, and hugs, and cookies. She spoke, a couple of times. Willing to try. The looks around the circle, the dense silence like hot concrete pouring over the room were another stomp on her aching broken heart. Until one day, she snapped.

"I'd *kill* all of you, burn all my money, cut my hands and feet... to have been lucky enough to hold my kid's hand as she peacefully *disappeared,* you lucky assholes!" was the tantrum that got her kicked out of the support group.

After that, the business thing was her last resort to find a reason to stay alive. Staying alive was the only real vengeance she could get, so she was going to hold onto it.

Ana gave it a lot of thought and, as she circled around the idea, nothing felt as appealing as a sex shop. In her younger years, she had sold sex toys in meetings ala Tupperware. She was happy in those days. The meetings were fun. She didn't make a ton of money, but she learned a lot. Opening My Pleasure's door would be opening to her past self again. A safe space for couples of all ages and genders, ready to explore their sex life alone or together. A place for excited, nervous, happy people with healthy sex lives to feel comfortable when they wanted to try something new. A haven for older women learning about their own pleasure for the first time.

Yes, *that* was what she wanted.

My Pleasure was a white, spotless, open space in contrast to the dark, intimidating sex shops one could see around in her teenage years. Some of those still existed, but the majority of them had been destroyed by the amount of free porn and online stores to buy sex dolls and veiny latex cocks. Ana stocked anatomically correct dick toys and fleshlights, but those were placed behind a wall so people walking past the shop wouldn't get their eyes stabbed. What one would see when walking past My Pleasure were just colorful round vibrators. Rubber ducks. Eggs. *Toy-looking toys.* She was very proud of her displays, and it brought her immense delight every time a woman, alone, entered the shop and bought something for herself.

It did keep her mind busy, after all. For the eight hours the shop was open, for the extra hours she worked on taxes, cleaning, and fixing every-thing around the shop, Ana managed to focus *only* on the task at hand. Life outside My Pleasure didn't exist. Darkness was a pocket of sorrow on her free hours that were, as predicted by her sister, scarce. Ana never took holidays. My Pleasure held brunches and parties on Saturdays. On Sundays, she visited Amaya's resting place with a bag of churros and told her daughter about her week. Then, she had lunch with her sister, friends, or family. Her system worked just fine to keep the blade out of her skin. But this type of young couple...

They dragged the dark inside My Pleasure.

The hairs on the back of her neck stood up as if a dangerous animal had entered her domains as soon as the bell rang. Goosebumps covered her skin. Ana looked at the couple with the same angst of those witnessing an inevitable accident. Her mouth drew a grin despite her best intention to keep her feelings under her *retail mask.* If she could, she would slap the girls, shake them to make them understand. Sometimes, when these types of couples came in, Ana fantasized with attacking the boys with the pencil she was holding. Jumping on them, forcing them to the ground, and stabbing their eyes again, and again, and again with the sharp pencil until it broke inside of their skulls. She could hear their screams in her head. Feel their blood soaking her clothes, taste it seeping into her mouth.

"See?" she wanted to shout to the girls covered in their boyfriends' blood. "See? This is the only way!"

Deep down, what really infuriated her was the fact that those girls were just as blind to all the tales as she had been.

"No hay peor ciego que el que no quiere ver," her mother used to tell her in their fights over Ana's husband's behavior.

Whenever these types of clients showed up, she couldn't stop the internal monologue. This was exactly what her couple looked like. Before it didn't look like anything resembling happiness. This kind were easy to spot, because while the girls were focused on *him*, on choosing toys *he* would enjoy, the boys took every chance they got to direct their glances at Ana. And all their looks said the same. The thirst. The "I would do you in the back while she shops" stare. The "this is about me" look. Her scars itched. As always, when they were done choosing an absurdly large latex cock and a male masturbator, nothing with so much as a hint of vibration, she slipped some information flyers about healthy sex, healthy communication, and relationships in the couple's bags.

Hoping.

It took all her might and then a bit more to not pick at the scabs when the boy touched her fingers, just barely but *intentionally* when handing her his credit card. *Asshole.* Once the couple left, Ana ran to the door. A panic attack was gathering at her chest. About to explode. She turned the friendly "I'm open" smiley pussy on the door to the "Closed" sleeping one with a nightcap sitting on its clit and ran to the back room.

Ana removed her sweater as if the wool was choking her. She took a good look in the mirror at the naked skin on her upper half, clenching the sink and counting how long her breaths should be. Her body was a tapestry of scars that covered all the skin not visible under a long-sleeved, round-collar shirt. When her chest stopped pounding, she turned around to contemplate the clean triangle of skin on her back, where her hands didn't reach. There was something mystical about it. Something hopeful about that piece of clear skin, an island rising among the pain.

Sometimes, she fantasized with someone engraving the words in that empty space and the thought always made her heart shrink, for she couldn't imagine herself being that intimate with anyone again in whatever remained of her life. Other times, she dreamt of longer arms and bending elbows so she could erase any kind of hope from her body. *You don't deserve hope. You don't deserve rest.* Trembling with anticipation, Ana took the scalpel out of a tiny black leather bag she kept in her purse and examined her body carefully, looking for the right spot. Tears choked her, and they had to be stopped. The child's screams inside her brain had to be silenced. The itch. The ache. The urge to slit her wrists open and let it be over with there and then. Right under her left breast, there was still some clear space. She lifted her breast with one hand and with the other, she delicately opened her skin, swallowing the soothing pain that transferred all her ache from her heart to the bloody surface.

As always when she wrote her martyrdom sentence in front of a mirror, it was all twisted. With some letters backwards, it would take the unknowing spectator a while to make out what the writings were. The last words her daughter said to her.

Cried to her.

Yelled to her.

Don't make me.

MAGDALENA

Magdalena jumped on the first bus to Vetusta early in the morning. It was her hometown, but it had been years since she last made that journey, and in the wee hours of the morning, it was breathtaking. The valleys. Snowed capped mountains. Rivers. Fog coming down the peaks, so thick it created a fantasy of cloudy lakes beneath the road. The drive to her homeland was beautiful, and it was a testament of the greatness of her God. She allowed herself to let out some tears of joy, to breathe in all that beauty worth saving from the night to come.

There was a reason she was sacrificing herself, even if it was difficult to remember it as she fled the safety of the convent. God's creation shone all around her, trying its best to remind her.

The gray and blue bus reached the large tunnel that conquered the mountains, the one separating the plateau from her parent's home. *El Negrón,* the locals called it. The big black. *A big black entrance to Hell.* The sun was shining bright above her when they entered the darkness of the tunnel, but after the long eight kilometers, the scenery at the other side changed dramatically. A dark, almost black, sky awaited her. Heavy rain struck the bus. Temperature plummeted.

No one batted an eye, as if that was completely normal. As if it wasn't the sign of the battle to come. Magdalena looked around. Kids were lost in their phones. Some passengers were asleep, and some were eating their sandwiches. The bus took a turn, and Magdalena looked back at the tunnel. Its mouth was pitch-dark, honoring its nickname. Magdalena's jeans suddenly felt damp. She wasn't used to wearing secular clothes; maybe the fabric was so rough against her skin that her childhood scars had opened, and blood would be covering her thighs. She looked down.

Snails moved over her legs, leaving slimy trails behind. Salamanders, golden and black, with their shiny skin, climbed up her thighs. Orange slugs had gathered at her crotch. She knew better than to think all those tiny creatures had somehow found their way onto a moving bus.

"El Diablo," Sor Magdalena muttered, holding onto the crucifix hanging from her neck so tightly the silver cross cut into her skin.

From her knuckles, crimson droplets fell to her jeans, drank fast by the fabric and the slugs. Her whole body was paralyzed by the clearness and realness of the apparition. She could even smell the mud, the earth, the damp in those slimy creatures' skin. Their weight on her legs, their movement over her was all too real. A stabbing fear broke through the nun's determination.

When the time comes, pain will feel like pain, even if it's just one of the Devil's tricks.

On the seat in front of her, the hat man stared at her with bright green eyes. This time, up close, his features revealed themselves to Magdalena in all their beauty. Wide nose, high cheekbones, and ample jaw. Green eyes and red hair. A soft peach down on his cheeks and chin. His lips were wet. Not a single imperfection on the skin of He who was once amongst the most beautiful angels, surely, for this couldn't be other than a demon.

"All creatures great and small." His voice resounded inside Magdalena's skull like an echo. His lips remained closed in a grin while his eyes spoke to her. "All whipped out as Earth burns..."

The nun instinctually stood up, holding out her bloodstained hand.

"Stay away!" she shouted.

Taking a step towards the apparition, Magdalena stomped over the creatures he had *gifted* her. The crushing of snail shells was almost as loud as her scream.

This time, everyone on the bus turned to look at her. As soon as the words left her mouth, the hat man was gone and, in his place, there was nothing more than a frightened teen removing their headphones.

"Ma'am, is everything all right?" the driver asked from the speakers.

"Yeah... No... Sorry, I guess I had a nightmare."

She sat again. Confused and embarrassed. Covered in sticky, cold sweat.

The heroic city was fast asleep in a winter nap when Sor Magdalena arrived at the bus station. Vetusta was gray and polluted. Noisy. Bursting with people running around looking down at their phones, blocking out the traffic with blaring music on their headphones. Christmas lights turned off during daytime only contributed to the cluttered atmosphere of the city. The same dark clouds that welcomed her back to her homeland gathered over Vetusta. But not even those were out of the ordinary in the North. The weather was dreadful two thirds of the year. Some rain wasn't a bother to anyone. Especially not around Christmas.

Nothing about Vetusta's streets, its buildings, or its people would lead anyone to believe it was about to be the epicenter of the Apocalypse. Just like Sor Magdalena didn't look at all like the flaming sword of God trying to stop it.

Yet, here we are.

Magdalena had been monitoring the killings of newborns and the profanation of churches closely around the world, and only Vetusta's numbers had skyrocketed in the last year. It would happen *there*. So, she knew *when*. And mostly *where*. She still needed a precise spot.

An invitation.

Walking around, wearing secular clothes, after over thirty years was extremely awkward. Even though there was nothing revealing about her outfit, covered by a thick brown jacket, the fact that her neck and long gray hair were exposed in her round collar t-shirt, that the jeans clang to her hips and thighs as if they were drawn over her skin, felt as wrong as walking naked around Sodoma. The only thing soothing her was the coldness of the tiny bloodstained cross against the burning skin of her chest.

At the station in Vetusta, Sor Magdalena carried a small squared brown suitcase, making it crystal-clear to anyone paying attention that this woman didn't come from the next town over but from a different planet altogether. She was travelling light, as she didn't plan on being alive in three days. Magdalena stood in the middle of the bus station, wondering if the Devil would be waiting for her outside the building. People grunted when they had to change their trajectories to avoid bumping into her. Magdalena's eyes refused to leave the floor, but she needed them to obey, to look around and find the exit door if she *really* wanted to fulfill her mission. How was she going to kill the antichrist if she couldn't even set foot into the real world because of some cheap tricks the Devil was playing on her?

Jesus had doubts too... She comforted herself. Being afraid wasn't shameful. And fear wasn't equivalent to cowardice. You could only be brave if you had been terrified before. A deep breath, and Magdalena was ready to go.

She knew every step of the plan by heart. After all, Magdalena had been preparing for it since she was eight years old. Back when everyone called her Verónica. A fierce girl afraid of nothing.

Or so she was before she encountered the archangel.

VERÓNICA

"I won't!" Verónica yelled at the top or her lungs, too close to her eldest cousin's face.

Playing damsel in distress again that morning was completely out of the question. She wanted to be one of the pirates. She knew damn well her screaming would throw Marcos off the cliff.

As expected, his response was immediate. Marcos pushed her hard and she fell to the ground. So angry had she been, so badly had she wanted to be on his face, that she didn't stop to consider the repercussions of her actions. Thinking ahead and not acting on impulse was not in her DNA.

It was the second week in their summer holidays as wild children in the country. As was the family's tradition, the four cousins stayed the whole summer at Abuela's place, and parents rotated helping their mother take care of her grandchildren. The agreement was perfect for everyone involved, including Nana, who got to cook and feed everyone as if none of the adults knew how to do it and were deliberately starving their kids and themselves. Food was that woman's only known love language.

That summer, life smelled of sunscreen, chloride, and tortilla de patatas instead of bleach, wax, and incense. It tasted like ice-cream and sea salt. Verónica's knees were permanently covered in scabs. Her hair tangled. Her shoulders sunburnt. Life was dessert and death didn't carry any meaning. The kids' favorite game in the village was scouting the woods around Nana's house, pretending they were explorers in the jungle. Or soldiers lost behind the enemy's lines. Warriors on an unknown planet after their spaceship wrecked.

It was Verónica's parents' turn to stay with them. That gave her the strength she lacked when her aunts and uncles were in charge. She wanted to be a fighter, not a princesita.

"Girls can't fight," Alberto, the youngest, said.

Tears run down Verónica's cheeks. Not sad tears, but angry ones. She was rabid. Fighting the three boys by herself was out of the question. Madness didn't completely obfuscate her senses. She swallowed her pride, got up, looked at the three boys, trying to curse them with the power of her eyes, turned around, and run up the hill.

No one chased after her.

"I hope you get lost, and we never see your face again," Alberto's voice sounded in the distance.

She ran, and ran, and ran, up, up, up, until her legs hurt, and tears, regretful this time, clouded her vision. There was a tree over there. She would stop when she reached it and rest. Find the way back home to her mother's hugs. To Nana's hot chocolate and kisses.

Verónica could almost touch the tree's bark when the ground beneath her feet disappeared, and the frightened girl fell fast down a hole in the ground. Her knees crashed against the rough walls. Her body was that of a doll bumping into roots and rocks that broke her skin and her bones so fast it didn't even hurt. All the girl felt was extreme heat.

That must be what matches feel like when lit, Verónica thought when her disheveled body hit the cold ground and she lost consciousness.

Moaning filled the darkness as Verónica abandoned her dreamworld. In the dark, falling was but a distant memory. Marcos pushing her to the ground, though? That was clear as day.

"Cabrón," she muttered softly.

Her pain deserved cursing for the very first time in her life.

It took Verónica a while to realize she wasn't with her cousins anymore. That Marcos wasn't going to be impressed by her adult insult, nor was she under the summer sky. There was no warmth where she rested. No light. No birds chirping or bugs buzzing. There was just coldness, the bitter taste of blood. Mud drying on her skin. Verónica tried to open her eyes, but she remained in the dark despite her efforts. The girl blinked and discovered they had been open the whole time she'd been awake. Fear finally got ahold of her chest when she recognized that the voice breaking the silence, the aching soft moans, weren't hers.

Something hard, pointy, moved beneath the cold mud under her.

"It must be bugs, it's just dirty bugs," she told herself.

Over her own internal monologue, a grunt was clear enough there was no denying it was a male voice.

A pleading male voice.

When Verónica's eyes adapted to the dark, she made out shapes, movements. The scarce light's reflection on teary eyes wide open. Dirty faces. The moaning grew louder beneath her. Around her. The girl tried to stand on her arms, but a stabbing pain crossed her leg and right arm. Her heart raced; she could see them almost clearly now.

Wounded men.

Soldiers.

Arms and legs bent in painful contortions. Still chests covered in steamy blood. Some of them dead. Some barely alive. Some under her, soaking her clothes with their blood. Verónica cried in fear. She had never been as terrified in her life. Those who could stand tried to climb the walls of the well, but they were slippery and stiff, so the wounded men kept falling back down, crushing their bones against the ground. Golden beam lights bathed them from above, moving around the hole like a lighthouse in the coast. Shadows of armed men looked down on them.

On her.

"I'm here," she cried almost inaudibly. "I'm... I'm here..." she tried again but her voice broke.

Black capes floated around the opening of the well, weird black hats projecting their distorted shadows on the walls like horns. A man in a long black robe appeared on the scene. A rosary dangled in his hands. A priest? He leaned over the well's mouth, and all the girl could make of his face was a grin with teeth so white they reflected the moonlight. His laughter fell down her prison in echoing circles. When one of them casted his flashlight onto the group, Verónica could see their green Guardia Civil uniforms. So, she tried again.

"Help me, I'm down here..." her voice loud and clear now.

"Rot already, rojos de mierda," the man with the rosary shouted with a giggle.

Why didn't they help her? Was she dead? Her body certainly ached like never before. Why weren't the wounded men surprised to see her there? To have a small child lying with them in the bottom of a death pit?

"Where are we? Who are you?" she tried to communicate with them.

They looked past her in the dark, though she was right in front of them. When the beam lights appeared again, and the very same shadows showered over them, when the same voice yelled:

"Rot already, rojos de mierda."

A realization hit her. Hard.

Those men where ghosts.

She was going to die down there if she wasn't already a forgotten corpse. Verónica screamed until all the air in her lungs exited her body, making her dizzy and confused.

The broken girl lay down and used all her strength to put her hands together in prayer.

"Jesusito de mi vida, eres niño como yo…" she couldn't remember the words Nana forced her to repeat every night. "Eres… eres niño como…"

Tears filled her throat and stop her words from coming out.

A ball of fire materialized out of nowhere, burning the corpses of the soldiers with a fire that didn't burn but healed her wounds.

A thousand burning eyes stared at her. The whitish blob radiated a warming golden light. Verónica's body ached no more. Frozen by fear and captivated by the splendor of the creature at the same time, she dared not move.

"Fear not, child," the creature said with a thunderous voice composed of a million tiny voices from the bottom of the ocean. Gurgling. Melodic.

Just a second before, Verónica was surrounded by death and misery, dying in pain, and suddenly she was gorging in the creature's soothing presence. The only logical conclusion was that she was dead. She had died. Fell, hit her head, gone to Heaven. Only this place was nothing like Heaven sounded like in Sunday school.

"You are very much alive, Verónica. Hear carefully: I have a story for you."

It took the adults three whole days and nights to find Verónica. Abuela never lost faith, she told the girl.

"I felt you," she said, embracing her granddaughter. "Te sentía en mi corazón."

She was told later that her cousins didn't know where she had run to; they couldn't point the search parties in any direction. Police closed the roads, controlling every car in case someone was trying to drive away with her. There were journalists camping in front of Nana's house since the very first night.

Apparently, it was her cousins, more adventurous than the adults, who finally found her when they tied a thick rope to the tree and slid down in hopes that she was just not able to listen. The other only possible option was that she was nowhere.

"Oh, mi niña, gracias Dios mío, es un milagro," Nana said, with tears running down her cheeks, when the firefighters emerged from the pit with the half-dead girl in their arms.

Verónica's cousins looked as if it had been them who had seen a dozen ghosts, who had been as close to death as one could get. Everything changed between them after that summer. Guilt must be eating them alive, the girl thought back then.

"We are sorry" was all they said when they visited her at the hospital.

"I forgive you." Verónica dug her nails onto the wounds in her leg.

She needed to. If she wanted to learn to be forgiving, to not sin, she couldn't be hating her cousins. And what for? They were only children, and it was an accident. Something made her innards boil in their presence. So, she had to hurt herself to make her own feelings go away.

She needed to be perfect.

Her soul needed be preserved, as clean as unused china, just to be beautifully broken at the right time.

Verónica was only half conscious during the three days the bright creature kept her under its spell. Hidden from the outside world, floating in limbo, she contemplated the doom of humanity. All the sins in the world but also all the healing humans were capable of. War and peace. Cruelty and love. Bloodshed and light. She wasn't of this world for three whole days and nights, so she didn't reply to the voices of her parents calling her name during their searches in the woods. She couldn't see the flashlights. The hounds sniffing down the hole on the ground next to the tree. There was only a distant song mixed with her memories of the mystical voice. The lyrics forged on her brain as the holy words.

"Al pasar la barca

Me dijo el barquero

Las niñas bonitas

No pagan dinero."

For three days and three nights, not only did she see the two possible futures awaiting humanity, but she also contemplated her future self. And El Diablo. And the night they would be one. The night he would trust her enough to make her a participant to the birth of his child.

In a world devastated by greed, lust, and pollution, her immaculate face would be the torch that would enlighten it all, that would clean the unclean. Giving knowledge back to humanity. Saving them all, the worthy and the unworthy. A second chance.

"Serás La Inmaculada. A promise made to humanity's best. A fire that would consume all human agony while it consumes itself."

The first day home after a full week in the hospital, fear took hold of Verónica's heart. What if she forgot any of the vital information that creature gave her? Humanity would be doomed if she forgot anything, just like she kept forgetting to do her homework or where she had put her color pencils. She was not going to let herself ruin this for everyone else. She thought about her parents, her friends, her grandma, who she still believed would live to be one hundred and twenty, at least. All their lives would be in her hands one day.

When Verónica was sure everyone was asleep, she sneaked out of her room and went straight to the kitchen. Barefoot, in her oversized summer t-shirt and underwear, she looked like a stick girl drawn by a toddler. The night was warm. Crickets sang outside. The night sky, usually covered in clouds, was clear, and moonlight bled through the big kitchen windows with a blue tint. Verónica took one of the knives from the cabinet and sat with her bare legs against the tiles. Slowly, she drew, on her thigh, the symbol the whitish blob had showed her. Almost a pentagram, almost a heart, neither of both and the two at the same time.

The cuts weren't as painful as she thought they would be. It was more of a tingling feeling in the back than the full-on pain of being kicked in the gut by a cousin. Like a marker, the knife drew red lines in her milky skin. To make sure the symbol would stick, she went over the lines over and over again, until it did hurt. Until bright blood flooded from the lines dripping from her thigh to the tiles.

She also wrote a date. The real vital piece of information. Her countdown. Verónica thought if she wrote a date, the adults would be able to tell its meaning. If she wrote how many days were left for her to stop the Apocalypse... Then, no one would know. No one would try to stop her.

"For love blinds," the light creature said.

Verónica was carving out the days when a voice whispered at her back.

"What are you doing, nena?"

It was Nana. In her long pink nightgown. Toothless as she was at night, with a white flowery nightcap on.

"Nada, Nana," Verónica replied hiding the knife at her back.

"I knew it was too soon for you to be coming back from the hospital, but no one ever listens to me." Nana approached her and took the knife. She helped Verónica stand. "Let's get you cleaned, nena. I told your parents, and I told the doctors. 'There're ghosts down there since the 40s, it's a gate to Hell, her sleep will be haunted. She still needs to rest to forget, but I'm just the crazy old lady.' Come on, child."

Verónica was moved by Nana's tears, yet sad she would have to leave her, all of them, soon. Eighteen seemed like a very long distance away before she fell in the well. It felt as if she would never be an adult. After her rescue, though? The ten years to go until her coming of age seemed like they would go in a blink.

And they did.

MAGDALENA

Under Magdalena's jeans, her childhood scars itched as if just opened.

When she was eight, she didn't fully understand what would be asked from her in her late forties. It was only the following year, during her first communion classes, that she was able to identify the flaming creature she had seen as an archangel. Her heart rejoiced when she saw the image on the textbook. All the eyes, the feathers, the light. There was no doubt.

Also, not sinning? That was easy to comprehend. But how could she know what a sex cult was back then? She barely knew about sex, let alone sects. She cried for a whole day the day she found out what cults were, watching Informe Semanal with her parents. But she sucked it up the next day and never shed one more tear for her own fate.

She had followed the plan so far. The remaining task was finding the cult's lair so she could infiltrate their ranks and sign her deal with the Devil. *Easy peasy.* Magdalena took a long look at her list of Vetusta's sex shops.

A journey to Hell had to start somewhere.

Light inside Magdalena's first sex shop—Girls! Girls! Girls!—was hazy. Distant saxophone music played from speakers on the counter. Some men rummaged through boxes full of discounted movies. The purple carpet on the floor hadn't been cleaned in years. Magdalena couldn't recognize the acrid smell, covered by air freshener. A skinny man stood behind the counter. The dark bags under his eyes and his unkept beard suggested a not-so-healthy sleeping schedule. Even as she approached the counter, she could tell he smelled like stale cigarettes and beer. Was he the owner or just an employee? *What would make someone want to open such an establishment?* The man stared at her intently. *That look.* Magdalena had only felt as disgusted when a Vatican priest visited their convent. During his sermons, that *holy* man had that very same hungry look on his face. His eyes were a hundred hands fondling her as he recited the scriptures. Intruding under her habit. The sex shop clerk smacked his lips and straightened. He seemed ready to jump on her.

Trying her hardest to put her uneasiness aside, Magdalena smiled and approached the counter, where the clerk leaned in, inspecting her breasts shamelessly. She blushed.

"Well, hello there," he said with a smirk. "Anything I could help you with?" The tone of his voice was more mockery than invitation.

"Maybe. You see, I'm looking for..."

Magdalena dragged her words as she looked around, trying to find the symbol on the walls.

"I'm looking for..."

She turned her attention to the man's tattoos in hopes she'd spot it so this would be it and she wouldn't have to go through this whole thing again.

"Anything you fancy?" he laughed, misinterpreting her stare. "These are not for sale, but you can sure rent them."

"No. Not interested, thank you. I'm looking for... a group?" The words cut her throat like swallowing razors.

"Hey, Moreno," the clerk, laughing, called one of the men searching through the movies. "This beauty here is looking for some *group* action."

A clean-shaven, squared-shirt-under-a-green sweater, chubby man turned around. He looked way cleaner than the clerk. His stare, though, wasn't. There was that look again. Unmistakable. Like a uniform they all wore.

"Sure," he replied, satisfied.

With every step he took towards her, the nun turned smaller and smaller. Magdalena feared she would disappear beneath this man's shadow, that she would be reduced to a dust spec. She certainly wished so.

"Look at you; you look firm enough for your age," the man said, introducing both his hands into the nun's jacket and groping her breasts without even an attempt at asking for permission, as if the nun's flesh was nothing but meat on sale.

Magdalena jumped back. The other men in the store abandoned their searches and admired the show, laughing, and murmuring.

"Oh, sorry, milady, you wanted a kiss first?" the stranger said, closing again the space between them.

He placed his hand on Magdalena's back, forcing her closer to him. With her stomach against his crotch, she could tell he was hard under his jeans. She had never felt a man's penis against her before. She shuddered. Fortunately, rage took over before he had time to kiss her.

Magdalena slapped him.

"Ouch!"

He let her go, looking more amused than angry. Magdalena ran to the door.

"Oh, come on, don't go, we can be gentle too!" the clerk yelled.

The men laughed behind her. Icy sweat run down her spine. Her heart raced. Panicking, Magdalena rushed out of the shop, convinced they would follow her. Panting, exhausted. Her whole soul yearned to return to the bus station, back to the convent. At her back, the men kept giggling until the big metallic door shut them off.

"Didn't find what you were looking for?" a man, leaning on the wall next to her, said.

The man in a black hat was there again. He took the hat in his hands and blew the golden dust out of it before greeting her and putting it back on. He wore a red velvet vest with no shirt underneath. His hands, covered in rings, were tucked on his black skinny jeans. On that freezing December morning, he didn't seem cold at all.

"Who are you?" Magdalena asked.

Obviously a demon, but which one?

"You know me," the man replied with a confused look.

He tilted towards her, caressed her cheek with the back of his hand, the cold rings scratching her skin softly, and sang, almost whispering, in her ear:

"Al pasar la barca, me dijo el barquero."

"Wait, that song..." Magdalena's brain lit up to the melody as fireworks.

Cold slipped into her bones. Her skin ached, burning. She was thirsty, and hungry, and submerged in darkness. The song replayed in her head in childish voices. Bones breaking. Salty tears. Blood. Mud. Daisies falling over her powerless mortal coil.

The man retreated, staring at her lovingly with his captivating green eyes.

"Las niñas bonitas, no pagan dinero," he sang with the sweetest voice Magdalena had ever heard.

Then, he turned to leave.

"Wait! Who are you?!" Magdalena yelled confused.

On his way away from the nun, the hat man grabbed a passerby's hand.

"Yo no soy bonita," the woman picked up the song where he left it.

Magdalena followed the woman onto the main street. Surrounded by people shopping, going about their days with bags full of Christmas presents and their hands holding overprized coffees, the woman touched a kid's hand.

"Yo pago dinero," the kid sang, holding his mother's hand and grinning at the nun.

The song bounced from one person into another, circling around her. Magdalena turned around on her feet, following the song. Dizzy, she stumbled and fell to the ground. The loud song hurt her head. A pair of soft hands covered in rings held her chin. The hat man kneeled in front of her.

"We are legion, *Verónica*," he said, and she shivered at the sound of her old name.

"I'm not afraid of you; the Lord is with me," she murmured.

The hat man smiled; dimples adorned his cheeks. It wasn't a pleasant smile. It was the forced smirk of someone trying to hide his anger.

He shrugged. "Sure about that?"

His hands that had been so gentle on her chin turned hard and pressed on her neck with a swift movement. Her feet danced in the air, holding on to the man's hands, he took her back to the narrow street, where Girls! Girls! Girls! pink neon shone. The hat man pushed her against the wall. Her skin burned under his touch. His breath smelled like sulfur. His loving green eyes turned an angry bright yellow. Snake eyes. Magdalena chocked.

"He doesn't give a damn about you. About ANY of you," he said in her ear.

"You are the father of lies," she whispered.

Magdalena took the cross out of her neck with a firm blow and pressed it against that demon's forehead. His skin hissed. The hat man screamed in pain and let her go. When she fell to the ground, she found herself alone again.

ANA

"First time?"

"Excuse me?" the anxious woman asked, startled.

Ana gave her a candid look, left the counter, and got closer. Slowly, not too fast, as if chasing a stray kitten. One misstep and that woman would run out of the shop never to be seen again. She had been crying: puffy red eyes, swollen face. There was something about her untamed gray curls, the way the woman felt uncomfortable in her own clothes. A bad divorce maybe? An escape from a life where she couldn't be herself? Whatever it was, a warm fire lit inside Ana, like finding a puppy on the street on a rainy day. The "I can be your shelter, your safe space" feeling. Ana experienced it many times since her daughter was taken from her. It had worked out fine sometimes. She had been taking advantage of in others. A few times, there was nothing she could have done to help. It takes more than one attempt to abandon an abusive marriage, but she was certain the time would come for those women to find her again. *Wishful thinking.*

"I know that look. It's the first time you've come to a sex shop, right? I'm Ana, the owner," she said with a gentle inviting tone.

"I'm Magdalena. I've already been to three different ones today... But I couldn't find what I was looking for," the woman replied.

Magdalena's cheeks burned, looking at her feet. Her smell —incense and wax—reminded Ana of Sundays when her grandmother dragged her out of bed, hangover and sleepy, to pray in the small chapel of her town. It was a miracle that this fragile being in front of her had kept going after trying other places.

"I figure you might need some help, then. Tell me, what is it that you have in mind?" Ana leaned against a shelf full of egg-shaped portable male masturbators.

Her black sleeves receded a bit, just enough to make some scars visible. Like magnets, they attracted Magdalena's eyes. Ana smiled and regained the straight position, hiding the scars. Pretending there was nothing to see. Nothing to say. Not to a stranger anyway.

"I... I'm looking for... a group," the woman said with exhaustion in her voice.

Ana almost laughed. *Bold choice for a first-timer.*

"Oh... Oh, I see." She wouldn't have thought, not in a million years, that a woman looking like she was straight out of a nunnery would be looking for a swingers' club, but she did have the information. "Here, I have some brochures, only of good respectable places I have checked myself. I wouldn't send my clients to unsafe environments, you know?"

They walked to the counter, where Ana took the brochures out of a drawer and placed them in front of Magdalena, who avidly held them, inspecting them very close to her face.

Ana waited. When she looked outside through the shop's big window, a tall man with a hat looked straight at her. It wasn't uncommon, and it always pissed her off. She walked to the window, smiling the fakest of grins. The man removed his hat and bowed. His eyes were so weird. Too bright. Too green. His red hair almost too red. He nodded at her with a gentle smirk, like he found her amusing. The look in his eyes was that of recognizing an old friend. It sent shivers down her spine. Fast, she closed the blinds before turning back to Magdalena, who was rummaging through the papers with a frustrated expression.

"Excuse me, but what is it you are looking for *exactly*...?" Ana asked, willing to shake the image of the man from her head. "I don't mean to offend you, but you don't look like the type of women who would be looking for a gangbang..."

"What's a...? No, I'm not. Not any of this, they don't have the symbol... It's not this..." Magdalena smashed the brochures on the counter and looked around in despair.

Her eyes were bright, watery, clearly, she had come to the end of a road and couldn't figure out what to do next.

"If you told me what you are looking for in a little bit more of detail, maybe I could—"

"I'm looking for..." Magdalena said, lost, desperate, anxious, "I'm looking for a cult... A sex cult... I figured I could start my search in a place like... this one."

Ana didn't appreciate the tone or the implications.

"But it's not... I thought the Lord would help me, that it would be easier, I thought..."

Oh.

So, this woman was a nut job. Ana, despite her life experiences, wasn't a good character judge.

"I'm afraid I can't be of any help," her tone dried.

Ana took the brochures from the counter and looked at Magdalena with her best "it's time for you to leave" look, perfected after years of working retail. But the woman didn't move. She just stared at Ana, more like *through* Ana, her eyes drifting away as if she was about to lose consciousness. The clerk went 'round the counter; in case the woman fainted, she would need to protect her very expensive crystal counter.

"You okay?" she asked, but Magdalena didn't even turn to look at her.

Her lips trembled. Like she was about to cry. Her cheeks red. Her skin suddenly sweaty. Her eyes closing. Her muscles tensing. Whimpers falling from her slightly open mouth. She was about to have a breakdown. *Or an orgasm.*

Ana got closer to Magdalena, grabbed her arms to shake her. Right then, the woman let out a deep moan, focusing on Ana's eyes. Yes, that was an orgasm and there was no mistaking it. There was no time to decide how that made her feel when blood dripped from Magdalena's wrists onto Ana's arms, onto the floor as she held on to the clerk. Her eyes, open wide, looked purple instead of dark like they had a minute before. Her blood didn't smell coppery but flowery. *Lilies.*

"Oh, wow, are you okay? Wow, wow," Ana held Magdalena by the shoulders.

"It's you; it's you," Magdalena muttered with a smile before passing out. "Your flaming heart..."

What the hell just happened?

Ana went from shock to emergency mode in the fraction of a second. Magdalena's wrists were two rivers flowing red, leaving the woman white as porcelain. There was not that much blood inside a body for this woman to survive Ana having any second thoughts. Time was the only thing that would make a difference. No time to call 112 and wait around for the ambulance to arrive while she paced up and down the shop, contemplating someone dying on her floor. That strange woman would bleed to death before anyone came to their aid, and her car was right there.

Magdalena appeared to be semi-conscious. Her eyes were wide open following the clerk around. Yet her body was limp lying on the cold tiles in a pool of her own thick blood. Ana kneeled next to her.

"Come on, love, we have to get you some help." Ana placed one hand under Magdalena's back and the other one grabbed one of her arms. At their first standing attempt, their sneakers slipped on the blood. "You need to help me, preciosa, please."

Preciosa was her favorite name to call her daughter. It slipped from her tongue. Smelling the flowery scent of the drying blood, Ana remembered the strong odor inside the church the day she buried her kid. So many people sent flowers that the smell turned from pleasant to pungent. Her mind went straight to the image of her child's small body gasping for air on a pool of blood.

The second attempt to lift Magdalena failed too.

"Come on, if you have anything to live for, you need to help me." Magdalena turned her head to Ana this time. Her body reacted and they managed to get up.

Magdalena allowed Ana to lead her, but in a distant way, her body was almost that of an automaton. People stared at the two women, but no one offered them help. Ana smiled at them with her most hateful smile as she struggled to open the back door and help the woman stand at the same time.

She placed Magdalena on the back seat and fastened her seatbelt. The leather belts she had knotted around the woman's wrists were not enough to stop the blood from soaking her car's seats.

Ana had never driven so fast around Vetusta before. A weird feeling tingled in her chest. She parked the car in front of the emergency room, although *park* was probably too good a word for what she did, and then rushed into the hospital.

"I've got a woman bleeding to death over here; we need help," she yelled.

Some nurses and doctors run to her help outside and took Magdalena out of the car.

"You can't go in." Someone stopped her when she followed them. "Go to the counter; fill this up," a woman said, giving her a folder and a sticker with the same numbers they have just stuck on a wristband around her mysterious costumer.

There wasn't much Ana could tell the nurses at the main desk, other than explaining what happened to raising eyebrows and confused stares.

"I already told you, all I know is her name is Magdalena and she didn't do that to herself, and I certainly didn't do it to her," she replied for the tenth time. "I have cameras in my shop, I can prove it."

"Well, we'll need you to stick around and talk with the cops, okay," the nurse told her in a very harsh voice.

Ana grinned her fake retail smile to the woman.

"Can I go outside or am I detained?"

The nurse smirked for all answer.

Although she had quit years before, Ana desperately needed a cigarette. Her heart rate was going back to normal. A replay of the scene showed up in her head. Weird and inexplicable as a dream. The woman in ecstasy. The blood. *All that blood.* The unnatural smell. Her whole body ached for a smoke.

A redheaded man was leaning on the wall, rolling a cigarette. Was he the same guy from the store? It couldn't be; there wasn't an aura of creepiness to him as was around the man on My Pleasure's window. She knew from all her true crime podcasts, a pastime lost after her child's murder, that incorrect eye witnessing was one of the main reasons people were wrongfully convicted, so she convinced herself this poor guy had nothing to do with the creepy shadow she had seen before. That it was all merging together in her head because of the stress of the whole situation, and this man, smoking outside an ER, probably had enough on his plate already.

"Hey, would you mind rolling me one? I quit a long time ago, so I didn't bring any... Fuck, I wasn't expecting to end up needing one today."

"Sure. Here, have this one. I saw you two coming in; the woman bleeding, she tried to hurt herself?"

"Oh, no, no. She didn't. It was... just a freak accident."

Ana wasn't planning on talking with a stranger about the weird thing she had just faced. She wasn't even sure where to start, or how to articulate her experience in a way that she didn't sound batshit crazy. That woman, Magdalena, must have had some injures in her wrists. Maybe she *did* try to hurt herself before; she certainly looked like a troubled mind in desperate need of help. There must have been some stitches in her arms that broke loose. *Right. Yeah.* That was a good explanation, and one Ana could live with. There was no way those deep lacerations opened by themselves out of the blue.

"I don't really know her; she was a costumer in my shop, and she had an... episode? I just brought her here instead of calling an ambulance."

"Oh, I see, she was lucky to find you then," he took a puff and smiled at Ana with pursed lips.

Being the subject of that gesture felt like stepping into a warm bath on a freezing day. Her soul brightened, and so did her cheeks.

"Everything happens for a reason, *Ana*," he said.

"How do you know—" Ana wanted to ask, but he threw his cigarette to the floor, and approached her in one swift movement.

His hand reached out for Ana's waist. The man was way taller than her, and so he had to lean in to gently caress her lips with his, kissing her with such passion Ana's heart almost stopped.

She should have slapped him.

Wanted to.

Instead, her body, every last living cell in her, felt compelled to get closer to this strange man. His body was burning fire. His tongue on hers was slippery, hot. Ana's sex was as wet as his mouth. Her legs trembled. She *craved* him. Her whole self drowned in the desire of his flesh. Not even her ex-husband, may he rot in Hell one day, had ever inflamed her like that. She ached to devour this man, to be devoured by him, and not in a metaphorical way. She longed to have her body completely destroyed by him. Drained of her blood, of her life, she would give it all to him. Take it all from him.

When Ana opened her eyes, she was holding thin air, the cigarette burning in her fingers. He was there. *Wasn't he?* She didn't make him up. *Did she?* Something moved in her mouth. Something warm, and big. Wet, anxious, choking her. Ana coughed. Whatever it was, it was trying to get inside her through her throat. Ana took her hand to her mouth and grabbed the slippery creature. She retched and coughed again, and a bright orange slug fell to the floor in front of her. Ana gagged, horrified. She looked around again, but there was no trace of the man.

"Ana López," a nurse called from the door.

She stomped on the slug and followed the nurse in.

Magdalena was discharged with some stitches in her wrists and a psychiatry appointment; Ana was sure the woman wasn't going to attend.

"They didn't think you should stay? Really? No offense, but you do look like you need some help if you—"

"I didn't try to kill myself. I explained to them how the accident happened, and they were satisfied with my explanation, once I came back to being myself," Magdalena replied.

Ana couldn't wrap her head around her encounter with that weird man. His taste still lingered in her mouth. Yet it must have been a product of her stress. Of her imagination. Being in that hospital where her daughter was born. Just a trick of her pain.

There was something weird going on. Something out of the ordinary. Something wrong. And dangerous. But the need to protect Magdalena grew stronger in her lower belly each second.

"Do you have a place to stay?" Ana heard herself asking before she had time to stop her own tongue, just like a while ago, when she couldn't command it to not kiss the stranger back. "I picked up your suitcase from the shop while I waited; it's not very heavy. Where should I drop you?"

"The truth is... I don't have anywhere to stay; I hadn't planned so far ahead... I'm ashamed now; you can drop me at the station; I'll find something," she said.

Ana took a good look at the woman, with her jeans, jacket and shirt covered in blood, her pale face and frail looks. Leaving her in the station would only add something else to the regret pile, because there was no way she would stay safe during the night.

"No way. I'm taking you home with me; we'll get you help tomorrow morning, and you can tell me your story while I get us something to eat. And drink, I certainly need a drink, don't you?"

"I don't drink. I've only drank the communion wine... I'm... I *was* a nun," she confessed, fastening her seatbelt. "I left the convent this very morning."

"Well, that's a first for my sex shop, I tell you..." Ana laughed and turned on the engine.

MAGDALENA

The two women drove in silence. Magdalena contemplated the city through the car window. The storm clouds were darker. More menacing. The night was tinted vermillion instead of blue. Christmas lights tried their best to cheer the dreadful night, but no amount of jolly brightness would change the feeling in the air. The wheels of the end of times were in motion.

This woman driving was a vital part in the divine plan. Her bones told Magdalena so, although something about Ana made her feel uneasy. She was at least ten years younger than the nun, but the pain behind her eyes looked a hundred years old. As she turned the wheel, her sleeves moved, allowing Magdalena to take peeks at her scars. Letters, she was sure of that. Her own scars itched.

"Home, sweet home," Ana said after parking. "It's a miracle we have found a parking spot this close to my place on the first try, you lucky charm," she joked.

Ana's voice was sweet. Too sweet. Pretending she hadn't witnessed Magdalena covered in blood mere hours before. It was only natural for Ana to think Magdalena hurt herself or tried to. Understanding the truth required faith. *Was that woman religious?* She couldn't be. Not with that job. Despite all her good intentions, would she be saved in the purge to come? That was only for God to decide.

Sad, still.

The nun paused for a second after closing the car door. A huge, modern, white, oversized building shaped as a dove reigned in front of her. Right in front of Ana's door. It was like someone hadn't taken the surroundings into account. That dove looked like it was about to devour the surrounding buildings.

In all fairness, it was not completely white. Constant rain had drawn orange tears on its walls. Black mold spots raised from the ground up. It looked old and abandoned, but such a modern structure couldn't have been imagined in any other century than the 21st.

As Magdalena was looking at it, big cold raindrops fell on her face. They ran over her cheeks and seeped into her mouth. They tasted sweet.

"A monstrosity, right? I got the flat way cheaper because of it, you can almost touch it from my balcony." Ana stood next to Magdalena. She held her hand out to check on the falling raindrops. They made muddied puddles on her palm. "Let's go inside; it seems it's one of those dirty rains."

Lightning struck the white building, sending sparks all over the wings. Thunder ensued, making the ground beneath their feet tremble. Magdalena's eyes followed the rain of sparks, falling like firework from the building to the ground. There he was. The hat man stood on the door of the building. Smoking. Though he was on the other side of the street, she could see his white teeth, like fangs shining in the dark, as he smiled at her.

Magdalena walked past the door, following Ana. Coincidences didn't exist as far as she was concerned, so this stranger had been put in her way for a reason. The Lord had plans for her. It didn't help the nagging sensation at the back of her stomach, a sudden repulsion when she dared think her mere presence was putting Ana at risk. She would have to ask more of her, take more, demand more. There wasn't any scenario in which doing so wouldn't mean condemning her savior's eternal soul. That feeling had to go. Love, compassion, were enemies in the battles to come. The archangel warned her about it.

"For love blinds," his voice repeated and repeated.

Magdalena had to push any compassion, any feelings, down. Down. Down until they were no more than the aftertaste of communion wine gone sour.

Ana's place had to be the most charming, beautiful home Magdalena had ever seen. Admittedly, she hadn't seen many since she was eighteen. The walls were painted in a deep dark green. Lamps and frames, golden. There were lush plants in the corner. No TV, but a nice vintage record player. Bookshelves went up to the ceiling, full of books of all shapes and colors. This wasn't at all what Magdalena expected judging by the exterior of the building.

The beauty was overwhelming for her. She had always lived in an empty cell, with little more than a bed and a broken nightstand. White walls without a hint a color. Yet, somehow, her cell had been more *alive*. Ana's place lacked warmth, like setting foot inside a museum display. Meant to look like a real home but obviously not one.

On the walls hung paintings of women and nature intertwined. You wouldn't know if they were becoming a part of nature or being devoured by it. That was their magic. There was not a single personal picture on display. Nothing remotely personal. The kind of ugly things people hung on their walls or place on their bookshelves because they meant *something,* anything, to them, more than an awful selfie in a train station or a wrinkled ticket. Even Magdalena, who lived her younger years secluded from the world, knew this.

Something caught Magdalena's curious eye while Ana took their jackets and her suitcase into the room. Right where most people would have a TV display, a shelf held as many pomegranates as one could imagine. Paintings. Collars. Pendants. Figurines. Dozens of them, each one redder and brighter than the other. Like porcelain blood splattered against the Victorian green wall.

Magdalena came closer, tantalized. Right in the middle of that pomegranate altar lay a wrapped-up box. Black, shiny wrapping paper with big red drawn poppies. The ribbon was golden and luscious. The last time she saw a present like that was her eighteenth birthday. Her heart softened, and for a second, she was Verónica again, excited to open a gift, even if it wasn't meant for her. Excited to sing one last happy birthday in her life.

"Oh, is it your birthday or just a Christmas present?" Magdalena asked, holding the wrapped-up box with a smile.

"No, it's... It's kind of a long story." Ana took the box from her hands and put it back in its place, all light gone from her face.

"Here, I got you some clean clothes, you can use the shower there, and I'll put those bloody clothes in the washing machine," Ana said, handing her pajamas so softly that Magdalena was immediately transported to her childhood, to the touch of her teddies.

"It looks beautiful and expensive, yet it's still unopened. There must be an important story behind it," she said while smelling the soft pajamas.

"No, sorry, I... It's not that long a story. It's just decoration."

Liar.

Magdalena unwrapped her wrists. As usual, they were already healed. She covered them again, nonetheless. Scaring Ana was not something she needed right then. *Not yet.* Her cheeks were rosy. She took the chance to put her necklace, her crucifix, back on her neck. Having her Lord resting on her skin gave her all the peace and bravery she needed. Magdalena hadn't realized how much she needed that shower until she set foot under the warm water. After a long time under it, she felt renewed.

"Thanks, I needed that; how do I look?" she asked Ana, turning around in her soft PJ's.

Ana didn't reply, she just smiled and walked to the kitchen. Magdalena followed her. That room was just as perfect as the living room and the bathroom. Was it ever used? The nuns were very diligent with their cleaning duties, and despite their efforts, their kitchen never looked so spotless. Some delivery boxes peeked from the trash can. Not caring enough for yourself as to cook a proper dinner to enjoy was an extremely sad thought for the nun. Food was the thing she missed the most in the convent.

"What would you like to eat?" Ana asked, unaware of the turmoil her unused kitchen had provoked on the nun. "It must be take-out; I don't have anything here. I wasn't expecting visitors."

"I don't know, what's your favorite? In the convent, we only ate what Sor Dolores cooked, and she wasn't into making food delicious. Gluttony is a sin."

Ana chuckled and pressed Magdalena's arm with a commiserating gesture that sent shivers down the nun's spine as she whispered:

"You're trying ramen noodles today. We need to warm ourselves."

Ana took their food order from the door and put the noodles into black bowls with red interiors in front of Magdalena, who looked at her plate a bit confused.

"Doesn't it look good?" Ana asked, holding the spoon, waiting for the nun to start eating.

It did look absolutely delicious. Magdalena's stomach growled at the savory smell, at the delicious look of the food in front of her. Gluttony was a sin. Magdalena had had a steady diet of not-very-tasty foods for as long as she could remember. The taste of her childhood dishes had dissipated; she couldn't tell what her grandmother's croquetas tasted like anymore. What the texture of her casadielles were.

"You'll like it, you'll see," Ana encouraged her, unaware of the nature of the doubts nesting inside the nun's heart.

Magdalena smiled and happily took the spoon to her mouth, and it exploded on her tongue like fireworks. All her senses tingled at the taste of the broth, at this new experience that warmed both her stomach and her soul. Her face turned red. Such a feeling couldn't be but sinful.

"It's good, right?" Ana chuckled.

"It is... It is good," she said with her mouth open forgetting her manners completely.

One. Two. Three. Four and five spoons. Half an egg that tasted like no egg she had tried before. Salty. Sweet. Juicy. Three times, she filled her mouth with noodles. A tiny piece of delightful pork that melted on her tongue. Magdalena would have eaten the whole thing and ordered another one. But she forced herself to stop there. She feared the pleasure she was experiencing would ruin her. She could imagine El Diablo laughing at how easy it was to trick her. Just a minuscule taste of the pleasures the mortal coil could experience, and she was lost. But no, she wasn't a weakling. Her mission and its conditions remained clear. Ana finished hers without talking, lost in her own thoughts.

"Hey," Magdalena said when Ana came back in the living room from the shower after dinner. "About that present: it's not just decoration, right? It can't be anything worse than bleeding out in front of a stranger..."

Ana hesitated. Magdalena spotted the struggle behind her eyes. With her curly black mane falling wet over her shoulders, without any makeup on, wearing red and green Christmas PJ's, that woman was the most tantalizing creature she had ever seen. *If you didn't count the archangel.* Magdalena looked away.

"I'm a nun," she pressed a little. "I'm sure I've heard worse."

45

ANA

SPRING, 2009

"How much do you love me?" Ana asked, her head resting on Antonio's sweaty, naked chest.

"To the moon and back," he replied, still catching his breath after the orgasm, caressing her face, tucking the wet curls stuck to her cheeks behind her ears.

"Only that?" she pouted.

"As much as the dark loves the light. As much as the moon loves the sun. As much as Hades loves Persephone," he murmured, as was their usual.

He declared his love for Ana on a letter with those very words, and they were now used quite regularly.

Ana curled up in Antonio's arms, soft like a kitten. That was her safe place. Warm. His arms were strong, and he always held her like he meant it. She had missed him. His lips. His beard. His chest. His hands. His cock. His breath. His tongue. Her heart beat so fast she wished it could explode into a tiny million pieces. Antonio straightened up in the bed, forcing her to do the same. He grabbed her by the arms and looked at her, dead serious.

"Promise you'll never leave me," he said. "I'll die if you leave me again."

"I won't ever leave you. I'm yours. If I were Persephone, I'd eat the pomegranate seeds willingly. I wouldn't only eat three; I would eat the whole thing," Ana replied, straddling him, holding his hands against the mattress.

"I would choke on them."

The cabin in the woods was his idea, and Ana couldn't have been happier. He wasn't the type to book holidays, so she was thrilled when he texted her to pack a bag and put enough food in the kitten bowl. It had been a rough couple of weeks for them since their last fight. María told her she should leave him, and she agreed while they were having coffee but only to make her sister shut up. How could she even think about leaving him? He was the only thing she could think of when they were apart. When they were fighting. She couldn't even understand what the fight had been about. And he didn't mean to hit her. She had thrown him to the edge. She knew she was tensing the rope too much when they were fighting, didn't she? He apologized immediately after. She shouldn't have overreacted and left as she did. He was crying and she left him there, alone, in pain, because she was surprised and weak.

As much as Hades loves Persephone, read the note attached to the tiny box the mailman delivered at her parent's doorstep that same week.

"Throw it away," María said when it arrived. "Don't even open it, the bastard."

But her sister didn't understand. Couldn't. She shouldn't have told her. Now she would only ever think of Antonio as the man who punched her sister. It wasn't that much of a punch either, was it? More like a slap?

Ana opened the box without replying to her sister.

"Fuck, I can't with you," María said and left the room, clearly annoyed.

It was a pomegranate necklace. The one dancing on Ana's neck as she made love to Antonio in that cabin in the woods he had booked to remind her that his love for her was undying. Immense like the universe. And he didn't mean to hurt her. It had been her fault.

MAGDALENA

Magdalena remained silent. No words invented by a human mind could express the magnitude of her anger.

"That's another first," Ana said, looking deep into Magdalena's eyes.

"What is?" the nun replied, coming out of her angry trance.

"I don't usually tell this story to anyone. I hate pity. I don't want to be pitied. It adds insult to injury, but there, in your eyes. That's not pity. That's... rage."

Magdalena looked at her, rearranging her face. As the end of times drew nearer, her feelings were multiplied ten times over.

"Why do you keep them up?" Magdalena asked looking at the pomegranates.

"A reminder? A punishment? I don't even know. Not always the same thing... So, not sure yet. The day I figure it out, you'll be the first to know."

There was something tender about this woman, who had been to Hell already and managed to climb out alive. Broken, but alive. Tender and kind enough to care for a woman she had just met. An immense urge to take her by the hand and tell her how important they were going to be took hold of Magdalena's heart. A need to tell her all about the bright future coming for humanity, where no woman would ever store porcelain pomegranates in her living room. A world without unnecessary pain.

It just occurred to her that, together, they might even survive to see it.

Magdalena insisted on cleaning the dishes. Although she couldn't find any cleaning supplies.

"El que cocina no friega," she said jokingly, as her grandmother used to say, opening cabinet after cabinet and founding them all half empty.

"I didn't cook anything," Ana protested, closing the cabinet doors the nun left open.

"You paid for it, same thing," Magdalena insisted when she finally found soap under the sink.

As she placed the bowls inside the sink and turned the warm water on, Ana grabbed her by the wrist.

"You can't get your wounds wet." She looked at the bandages that were too clean to be covering recently open wounds. "Can we talk about what happened now?"

ANA

"The stigmata. You have to be kidding me." Ana stood up like the couch was on fire.

She walked towards the window, unable to even look at the nun without feeling the urge to either kick her or run to the bathroom to take the scalpel out. *Always the same mistake.* Her scars itched. At least her daughter remained a secret to the stranger in her living room. Ana wouldn't be able to forgive herself is she had given Amaya, the agony of her loss, away so easily. Magdalena had to go. *Immediately.* Yet Ana stood looking out of the window, eyes glued to the white rusty walls of the building in front of her balcony without so much as opening her mouth. *The Antichrist, in Vetusta, for fuck's sake...*

"I know what you are thinking—" Magdalena said to her back.

"I seriously doubt that," Ana interrupted her without turning.

"You were there. You *saw* it happening. You *saw* the wounds up close, didn't you?"

"Of fucking course I did; I put those leather belts on you so you didn't bleed to death, so you could come into my house and con me? What is it you want?" Ana's words were harsh, all control over her tone of voice was gone.

"Turn around," Magdalena pleaded.

Ana didn't move a muscle. She didn't want to, because that would mean facing the indisputable fact that she had been tricked *again*. There were footsteps approaching her. Magdalena's warmth reached her back. Ana's spine tingled at her proximity. The nun's hand on her back forced Ana to close her eyes and take a deep breath. Why did this woman's touch have that effect on her? With her eyes still firmly shut, Ana couldn't tell what that sensation was; was Magdalena sliding her arms under Ana's? Was she trying to embrace her? The nun's breasts grazed her back. Ana's heart fluttered against her will.

"Look," Magdalena said with her arms outstretched at both sides of Ana's chest.

Ana opened her eyes, not because she wanted to look, but because she was at the end of her rope. Touching someone like that without asking first? Without so much as a hint that the physical contact would be welcome? She would throw this woman out of her house. Yes, she would kick her out despite the fact that she didn't have a place to stay. Was that even true? The words were ready to jump from her tongue, but they all fled once Ana's eyes laid on Magdalena's wrists.

Not only were the bandages gone but so were the wounds. The nun's skin was as smooth as if it was brand new. Soft and milky, perfect, not even a mole in them.

"That's impossible." Ana grabbed the nun's arms, turning around without realizing they were too close to each other. She drew lines with her fingers where the wounds had been. She had seen them, pressed her hands against them to stop the bleeding while she figured out which one of the leather belts on the shop would do the trick better. The warm, soft contact of Magdalena's skin on Ana's fingertips tangled her guts. She tensed, let go of the nun's arms and took a step back.

"The wounds went right through," Ana muttered puzzled.

She let herself fall to the couch. Was she finally losing her head? After all she had gone through? After all the nights she spent hoping for her mind to break completely so she would be oblivious to her own pain? Now that she had found balance, was this the time her reason failed her? Magdalena leaned in front of her, resting her pristine wrists on Ana's legs. Her heart shrank. She looked into that strange woman's eyes and couldn't find lies in them. Only hope. Only love. Ana recognized inside her belly a feeling she thought would never come back.

Yearning to kiss someone.

"This is God's work, a sign, for both of us," Magdalena whispered with a smile. "We'll stop the Apocalypse. Together."

Ana was a woman willing to believe. She had found no reason to do so before or after her daughter's death, but she ached for that bliss. Other grieving mothers in her therapy group had found solace in the fact that someday, sooner rather than later, they would be reunited with their kids in Heaven or whatever version of that they believed in. Lacking that certainty was another layer of hell in her life. The absurd notion that, just as she didn't exist before the night in the cabin with her ex-husband, Amaya had gone back to oblivion was too much to bear without even a hint of hope.

She longed for it, but she didn't have it in her. You couldn't force faith. You couldn't pretend or fake it. Either you had it, or you didn't. Even the tiniest doubt tainted that feeling, like a blanket that doesn't cover your feet. Never comforting enough. Witnessing a woman's wrists open as if pierced by a nail, only to be completely healed only a matter of hours later, was a good starting point for the believing journey because she couldn't find any reasonable explanation for what her own eyes had seen. Not just her eyes: her clothes were on the washing machine, covered in blood. Her sneakers. Her fingernails still had some of this woman's blood under them. It had been real. Her fingers had touched the wounds.

One single tear escaped her eyes. Magdalena held her hands and kissed them but immediately released them and stood up. Ana sniffled and took the glass of wine from the table where they had been dining and drank it in one gulp.

"Why you? Why me? Why here? When?" Ana asked; there were just so many questions popping out in her mind all at once. Her voice broke and she stopped asking.

"You might want to open a wine bottle."

MAGDALENA

Two empty bottles of wine rested on the living room table. The nun was impressed with her host's drinking ability. She didn't appear to be completely drunk. Just tired. Relaxed and willing to believe.

It was the first time she recounted her story, her mission, out loud since she met the archangel at eight. Forty years is a long time to keep a secret. Sharing it felt good. Sharing it *with Ana* felt right. Not being completely alone in the knowledge of humanity's pending demise was a relief.

"I don't know about you, but I don't feel like sleeping yet," Ana said, dragging her words a bit. "Not after all you've told me. Not after the day we've had. Wanna watch something? I don't think you had many chances to watch TV in the convent? It would put our minds to rest a bit. We'll need it if we want to be at our brightest tomorrow to find your sex cult."

"Some of the nuns did movie night on weekends, but I didn't watch them. I was sure the movies would... tempt me."

"And you want to keep it that way?" Ana asked.

"No, I'm supposed to get comfortable with sinning, remember?"

"I don't think some Friday night TV would do much harm anyway." Ana chuckled. "It's so rubbish it doesn't even constitute a sin."

Ana turned the TV on and started going through different channels. The TV light flickered on Magdalena's eyes, but she wasn't all that impressed. Until she spotted it.

The symbol.

"Stop!" Magdalena screamed, jumping from the couch. "Go back!"

Surprised, Ana did as she was told, and a woman doing a tarot reading came back to their TV screen. She must had been in her early sixties, and she was inside what looked like a church. A very gothic and well-prepared setting. This woman looked more like a horror movie night host than a charlatan. She had long grey hair, carefully curled. Cat-eye makeup and a black dress leaving little to imagination, however it didn't look like fast fashion at all. Her stiletto nails were classy despite the length, and her voice was soothing as a siren calling.

Magdalena got up and really close to the TV, frustrated.

"Can you go back to the beginning?" She looked at Ana.

"Yes, we can restart the show if you'd like. You know, the intro is pretty decent for late night TV, and she looks just like a gray-haired Elvira; I don't think you know Elvira," tipsy Ana rumbled. "You know, she came out recently; it was—"

"Stop! Stop there! That symbol," Magdalena pointed out. "That's the symbol the archangel showed me," she yelled when a mixture of a pentagram and a heart appeared on the big screen with the name of the show: Aurora's Sight.

Magdalena stood there, in silence, glued to the tv. It was all coming together. Every piece of the puzzle was falling into place. She was a fool for doubting even for a second that the Lord wouldn't help her. A couple of nursery rhymes and bugs and the Devil had her in his grasp. She needed to toughen up.

Ana didn't say anything.

Magdalena turned around. Dead serious. She wanted to prove that her vision wasn't wrong at all. That it wasn't a coincidence that they happened to see Aurora's show. She unzipped her jeans to Ana's alarmed expression.

"What the hell are you doing?" the clerk asked.

ANA

Magdalena rolled down her jeans without saying a word. She had big grannie peach panties one size too big. Her legs hadn't been shaved, and it was evident that under her underwear, she had never even so much as trimmed her sex. Ana had had too much wine to bear all that was going on. Magdalena put one leg over the table, showing her scars to Ana.

"See, here, this is what I saw when I had my calling. That symbol, a date... Two days from now. Well, one now," she said, looking at the clock marking way past midnight. "Everything the archangel showed me. We need to get to that woman."

An immense urge overcame Ana. Her scars itched. It was as if someone had tuned in a radio. Screams filled her head. Child's screams. Amaya's. She tried so bad to get rid of them, to reply to Magdalena, but she couldn't. She remained seated. Looking at the nun's white scars. Thinking about hers. Feeling hers. With the images of her daughter dressed in the communion dress she didn't get to use stuck in her head for no reason.

"She's the one that will take us to the cult..." Magdalena turned to look at Aurora on the frozen screen.

Ana looked away, outside the window the redheaded man from the hospital was looking inside. At her. He was there as if they weren't on the fourth floor. The taste of his tongue, of the slug, came back to her. The screams in her head turned unbearable. Fear got a hold of her chest. *It's just the wine. Just the wine.* What if everything the nun had said was really real? All the wine she had drunk didn't allow her to think clearly. Did she believe the woman? Did she just want to believe her? Was she infatuated with her? Willing to believe anything as she had done with her ex-husband? She shook her head to get rid of what she was sure was just her mind playing tricks on her, but when she looked back at the window, he was still there. Floating outside her window. Smiling.

"Excuse me." She got up and run to the bathroom.

She was going crazy. Everything was crazy.

Ana leaned over the toilet and her stomach contracted. Her vomit was red as blood, for her body was getting rid of all the wine she had drank. When she was empty, she lay on the cold tiles with a sweaty forehead and a vile taste in her mouth.

"Shut up, preciosa, shut up, shut up," she murmured to the yelling voice of a child in her head.

This feeling was too familiar. A panic attack was about to take hold of all her body. It was too much. Ana stood up. She removed her pants, opened the cabinet, and took one of her razor blades. Ana sat down on the toilet. Spread open her legs. There was a good spot on her thigh. There was some space left, but not enough. She didn't care. She was writing over old scars. With trembling hands, she wrote DON'T MAKE in capital letters. She let out a sigh of relief. The familiar pain soothed her soul. Two letters remained unwritten when the door she had forgotten to lock opened wide.

"We need to get there; we need to get to... her," Magdalena stated from the open door, with her eyes glued to Ana's bleeding thigh.

One Day

ANA

The fortune teller's studio was easy to find. Anyone with a computer could have done it without much digging. Ana was sure hordes of fans stalking Aurora were not an issue, so there was no point in hiding where you could send your snail fan mail. Those late shows were meant for desperate women on the verge of divorce, men unable to find a job, people in love who wanted to hear their twin flames were just playing hard to get.

Aurora, the tarot reader, recorded her show an hour away from Vetusta in an abandoned holiday city for working class families that Ana knew well. When she was little, her mother used to make bocadillos de tortilla and filetes empanados on Friday evenings so they could take the early morning train to the coast on Saturday and get a good spot on the beach. There were lots of rainy and gray days in the North even in the summer when Ana was little, certainly more than there were then. It wasn't by any means as hot and bright as Levante was, so not many tourists came to clog its beaches. Not everyone appreciated that the place was captivating when summer storms were coming. A mixture of golden light and black clouds. The smell of incoming rain mixed with sun cream and cooking meat.

But the place looked nothing like it did back then.

Small one-story houses with plenty of grass and space between them, two beaches with water so clear you could see fish without googles or putting your head underwater. There were barbecues for public use, a couple of bars, laundry building, church, infirmary... and a small halt, right at the entrance. It was the stuff of dreams for families in the '80s and '90s. Now it could very well be a horror movie scenario. That December, the twilight was gloomy, the tide high and the sea mad.

The bar, visible from the parking lot, was empty. Closed for good. Abandoned, if one were to guess. Some old red plastic chairs laid in a pile against one of the walls. Covered in rotting leaves. The public showers around it leaked orange tears.

That was a ghost town.

"What happened here?" Magdalena asked, looking incredulously at the small houses surrounded by fences and barbwire, half demolished, half engulfed by nature.

"Those were houses for workers, but at some point, they changed hands and now the government has them and hasn't been able to sell them to anyone. It's a pity," Ana replied, realizing she hadn't been back since her mother died.

She never took her daughter to that beach.

How could she not?

The thought stabbed her. Even if the houses were abandoned, they could have had small picnics there, just the two of them. Amaya could have learned to swim in the sea, just as she did. Ran around. Played with other kids in the sand. Being reminded of a new thing her daughter would never get to experience was the most painful of feelings. Things she would never do for the first time. Things she would never learn to do. Amaya would never drive. She wouldn't be kissed for the first time. She wouldn't fail an exam she had been studying hard for. She would never be fired. Never have her heart broken. The thought gave Ana pause, and she had to close her eyes and take a deep breath to control the tears. She should be at My Pleasure. Busy with orders and clients, with her mind

away from her daughter and the unfairness of her death. Away from the pain. From the guilt. The hangover wasn't helping much.

In the blue twilight, neither of them saw the homeless man walking towards them with a carton of cheap wine in his hand until he was right next to their car.

"Al pasar la barca." He grinned at Magdalena.

His eyes were bright when he turned to look at Ana. He stopped and grabbed Magdalena's silver cross. Up close, his eyes were just as green and bright as those of the redheaded man. He smelled of alcohol and urine. With a thud, he took the necklace from her.

"Hey!" Ana protested, pushing the man away from them. "Give it back!"

"It's okay," Magdalena whispered, caressing her neck. "I had to take it off anyway..."

The man, holding the cross for them to see, kept his eyes on them, walking backwards to the halt. Singing each verse louder than the first. He was almost screaming the nursery rhyme by the time he started walking up the stairs backwards.

"We need to rush," Magdalena urged her, grabbing her by the jacket.

"What was that? That song?" Ana asked.

"I'm sure it's something I heard when I had my calling... We really *need* to find that woman, now," Magdalena insisted.

Ana led the way, following a dirt path alongside the coast. She wasn't sure she remembered where the church was, and they had to retrace their steps a couple of times, but finally, there it was.

Against the black sky, the triangle-shaped church reigned alone, facing the road instead of the sea behind it. Red brick walls and big white windows. A huge, black, metal cross at the entrance pointing to the sky, right at the middle of the cusp of the building. Grass had overgrown on its surroundings, but a beaten path made it obvious someone got inside and out often. It had to be Aurora.

Ana's mother wasn't religious, so they had never been inside. She was curious as to how the tarot reader had managed to turn it into a recording studio or if she even had permits to do so. She must have, although there was always a chance no one simply cared. It was often the case in her region that people got away with this kind of thing because authorities didn't really give a damn about it. And, well, Ana thought, she was harming no one.

There was a dim light inside the building. Dancing. Golden. Candlelight. As they got closer, a figure appeared against the door. She lit a match and leaned on the doorway. Aurora was there, smoking a cigarette and looking at her visitors. She was still wearing the dress they had seen on tv an hour before. If she aimed to look like a witch, she had succeeded.

"Hi, are you Aurora, the tarot reader with the tv show?" Magdalena asked urgently.

They still couldn't see her face clearly in the blue light of the early morning hours.

"Who's asking?" a raspy voice replied, putting out the cigarette.

"I'm Ana and this is Magdalena, and we were wondering if we could get in and talk to you about something you might find... interesting," Ana said with her best retailer voice.

"I want to join..." Magdalena almost yelled.

Ana grabbed her arm and tried to stop her. It wasn't the way to start that conversation. But Magdalena shook her and with long steps got closer to the woman.

"I want to join your cult."

"What cult? I don't know what you are talking about." Aurora laughed at Magdalena's statement, then turned around to get inside her church.

As she was closing the door, Magdalena jumped forward and put her feet between the door and the wall.

"Look, lady, whatever it is you want, you can call tomorrow; it's late, and I need to rest," Aurora said from the crack in the door.

Ana noticed she wasn't pushing to close it either. This couldn't be the first time someone showed up at her door with some crazy story about the end of the world; maybe she found it amusing or enjoyed having fans knocking at her door. If you had a tv show and looked like her, you certainly love yourself some attention.

"Soy La Inmaculada." Magdalena's voice was firm. Blunt.

In the day they'd been together, Ana hadn't heard that determination yet. The nun could be fierce.

Aurora opened the door again. She looked at Magdalena from head to toe. Curious. Her interest piquing. Still, she didn't allow them in.

"Go on," the woman said, crossing her arms.

"I've lived in a cluster convent since I was eighteen years old," Magdalena continued.

Aurora didn't look impressed at all.

"There are lots of stuff people can do before eighteen, and I've met nuns that would put the Marquise to shame." She chuckled.

Magdalena blushed, but her voice didn't drop the fierceness.

"I've never in my life sinned since I took my first communion," she replied.

"I'm sure you've had crushes, a kiss, something you really wanted and another woman had; you must have hated another nun for not scrubbing the floors with enough pietas." The tone in that woman's voice infuriated Ana, yet Magdalena didn't even flinch.

"I'm ready to give you all the blood you need, and I'm willing to offer my eternal soul to your Master." Magdalena kept going. "If you're not interested, I'm sure we can—"

"Okay, come in. You have ten minutes," Aurora replied, opening the door wide.

She allowed the women inside. As Ana was closing the door behind herself, she saw, in the corner of her eye, a car, parked in the middle of the dirt road, with red lights on and a shadow inside. She was completely sure it was the redhead sitting in a car, even if she could only see his silhouette. He was following them. Was he even real? She turned around, walked outside, but one blink and he wasn't there. The car had vanished. The hair in her neck stood up.

"Everything happens for a reason," a voice murmured close to her.

His warm lips on her ear were as real as the cold of the wind in her face. The same unnaturally appealing warmth came from his body as the one she'd felt at the hospital. He provoked the same uneasy feeling when he had hovered on her window just hours before. His hands, with long, blackened stiletto nails, grabbed her arms. Her skin burned. He smelled so good it was intoxicating.

"Except Amaya's death."

Up close, she could see his teeth were sharp. Abnormally sharp. They didn't look like a cat's fangs, nor even a dog's. It was as if they had been broken to look like that. As if they were once perfect, and he had done that to himself. Chipped and imperfect. More painful even to imagine them on your skin, but she couldn't help but do so.

She closed her fist ready to punch him.

"Don't you dare say her name," she grunted.

Her fist only met the air in front of her, for she was alone again, in front of Aurora's church. Her skin showed red finger marks. Aurora peeked from the door.

"Tick tock, those ten minutes are running out, and she won't speak until you are here, so... you coming or what?"

She suddenly seemed very interested in what Magdalena had to say.

"Yes, yes, sorry, I thought I saw... someone."

"There's never anyone around here, amiga," Aurora replied. "Just the ravens and me."

MAGDALENA

The church wasn't anything like Magdalena would have imagined from the outside. It didn't look like the ones she'd prayed inside before. It was colder. Empty despite it being full of Aurora's stuff. God hadn't been inside those walls in years.

It was fairly small from the outside. Aurora had managed to turn it into a very gothic, very aesthetic, home slash recording studio. Magdalena's scars immediately itched the second she crossed the door. The *heartacle* was drawn all over the walls visible on Aurora's camera frame. The smell of incense was dense, mixed with flowers and something musky the nun didn't recognize.

"She's here, see?" Aurora said when she came back followed by Ana. "You can start talking now," she added, sitting on a green leather couch and putting another cigarette to her mouth.

"Are you going to smoke inside here?" Magdalena asked, perplexed.

There were many things she wasn't used to about the real world, the world she met outside the walls of her convent, and smoke was one of them.

"It's my home, so yeah. Time's running out, monjita," Aurora pressed, turning to Ana to make sure she closed the door.

The smell of the cigarette took her back to her childhood the second Aurora took that first puff. It was her father's smell. Nana's kitchen during sobremesa, when the adults had coffee and orujo and lit their smokes to just talk while the kids played. It gave her pause. But she composed herself.

"I'm La Inmaculada, the one that was promised to your people, and I'm here to offer myself willingly to your Master, so you can fulfill the mission of delivering the Antichrist on tomorrow's ceremony." Magdalena had to make sure that woman understood she was up to date on their plans.

She just needed access.

"That's a bold claim. La Inmaculada isn't more than a myth. Poetry. A figure of speech..." Aurora told Magdalena.

"What's La Inmaculada; what's that?" Ana asked.

"A woman so pure the Devil would grant anyone sealing a pact with her blood anything they want without having to sell their own souls," Arora replied. "Imagine a being so pure, just a fraction of their soul would be payment enough for the Dark Lord. So your friend here claiming she's it... Don't get me wrong, I'm still interested in knowing how you both came across that myth, and all the rest you claim to know."

Ana stood between Aurora and Magdalena, her eyes wide open, holding herself as if she was freezing. Magdalena had to admit she hadn't been completely sincere with her; despite trusting her, she hadn't disclosed the most dangerous part of her mission. Telling someone God and the Devil exist and that you were supposed to kill the Antichrist was already asking too much. She hadn't told her that it would be her sacrifice, the condemnation of her eternal soul through the most horrific of sins, that would save humanity and not just the killing of the spawn. She was afraid Ana would try to stop her. They only knew each other for one day, and yet the archangel's words, for some reason, felt like they would apply to her more than anyone else.

For love blinds.

"It's not. A myth. And I know you believe in it, even if you want to pretend you don't. We both know time is of the essence." Magdalena was savage, determined. "When the time comes, it would be way better to reign alongside your Master with your soul intact that being the tiles He walks on."

Nothing to do with the scared mouse she'd been all her life. The lioness had been dormant and was finally awake.

"I don't know what you are talking about," Aurora insisted, firm in her corner.

"Oh, come on, you stop playing this stupid game," Ana interrupted, exasperated.

"I seek you because I want to offer myself to El Diablo." Magdalena took a step towards Aurora. "Are you really going to turn down the present every other satanist on Earth aches for when it shows up in your doorstep?"

There was silence for a moment, while the woman pondered her words carefully.

"And who would you be in this scenario?" Aurora asked Ana.

"She came to my shop and…" Ana looked at Magdalena, who made a small gesture for her to keep the stigmata out of the conversation. "For some reason, I believe in her," Ana replied without taking her eyes off Magdalena.

Aurora squinted, looking at her like Ana was nothing more than a tiny spider under her gaze. Something about that scrutiny made Magdalena shudder. She suddenly felt left out of a shared secret. Aurora smirked at Ana, delight in her features, and turned back to Magdalena.

"I'm bored, and it's almost morning, so I'll humor you on this… because there's one way to know if you are full of shit or not," she said. "We will ask Him. If he shall come to our calling, then…"

"Then you'll take me to the ceremony tomorrow," Magdalena said firmly.

Aurora turned her head to the side; it looked as if she was listening to someone whispering in her ear, and she stood in that position for a while before turning to the nun and talking again.

"I'll take you both. If *she* wants to see *Amaya* again."

Ana shivered. She hadn't even told Magdalena about her daughter, not even mentioned she had one, let alone that she died or how. She hated hearing Amaya's name from a stranger's lips.

Magdalena glanced over her shoulder, and her eyes met Ana's teary ones.

"Amaya? Who's Amaya?" Magdalena whispered.

There was betrayal in her voice. As if she believed Ana's little snippet of her own history was all there was to know about her.

"I... I don't like talking about that." Ana closed the matter without even looking at the nun. Eyes nailed to Aurora. Screaming in silence for her to shut up.

A man's chuckle startled Ana. It was the redheaded man in the corner. She took a step back and almost lost her balance.

"Is everything okay?" Magdalena asked, looking at her and to the corner where Ana's scared eyes were fixed. Aurora didn't look back but smiled, complacent.

"She's okay. It's only that she likes her secrets," Aurora reassured Magdalena.

"Fuck you!" Ana screamed and ran out of the church.

How could Aurora know? Why was she hallucinating with the redheaded man? Was He the devil himself? Could that even be? Believing was way harder and more painful than she thought it would be. Believing wasn't the balm the other mothers pretended it was. Believing meant there was a God and that God had been okay with Amaya dying a horrible death at the hands of her own father.

Ana ran to a tree and collapsed there. Crying. Hyperventilating. Her lungs tight. She was rabid. Infuriated. With God? The thought made her chuckle as she fell to her knees and tried to catch her breath. She was so sweaty she feared all her old scars had opened. She feared being soaked in blood. The screams in her head were so loud Ana thought it might explode. God had heard those screams. God had allowed those screams to come out of an eight-year-old girl's throat.

A hand on her shoulder. Then fingers in her shirt's collar pulled slowly the fabric, surely unveiling her scars.

Don't make me.

Don't make me.

Don't make me.

All written in whitish skin. In other circumstances, she would have tried to stop that hand from intruding in her secrets. But she lacked the strength. Her soul wanted to be comforted by Magdalena. Her rage needed to be contained, for it was stronger and more dangerous than her pain.

"Your kid died? You didn't tell me, why?" Magdalena asked.

"I don't like talking about her..." Ana replied, hiding her face from the nun.

Again, it wasn't the whole truth. It was guilt that tied around her throat every time she tried to talk about her daughter. It had been her fault. No matter how many people told her otherwise, deep down, she knew.

"It was your pain that led me to you, don't you see? My stigmata opened when we met because of your grief, your suffering..." Magdalena looked around to make sure Aurora wasn't at hearing distance. "In the battle between Good and Evil, you'd play a vital role. Our Lord wants *you* to help me."

Our. Ana scoffed.

Ana cleaned her tears and walked back into the church with Magdalena. Her blood burning with rage. *Good and Evil.* What did that *Lord* know about good or evil. Ana didn't want Magdalena to notice her anger. Maybe, maybe she really was meant to have a part in the resolution of the Apocalypse, just not the one the nun had hoped for.

Aurora was waiting for them, collecting items from her witchy shelves. She didn't even turn to look at them.

"Amaya's not in Hell, just so you know," Aurora said with a firm voice as soon as they entered.

Ana's heart shrank. The unspoken fear, the one she hadn't even confessed to herself since Magdalena dragged her into that realm of believers, was just cleared by Aurora. Amaya never got to have her first communion. She tried the dress. She took the classes, but she didn't have the chance to have her last confession. It had never before bothered Ana. Relief calmed her down a bit.

Then, with her arms full of herbs, and crystal jars dinging, Aurora turned around to look at Ana with a smile.

"His Majesty is not interested in murdered children," she whispered. "Despite what the other side would love to believe."

Ana nodded. Aurora grabbed her hand and pressed it. Anger relaxed in Ana's heart; it softened. That woman's touched drained it, lifted it, and carried it for her.

"Okay, we'll do it as soon as we eat something. You can't summon the Devil on an empty stomach."

MAGDALENA

There was a small town at walking distance from Aurora's church. People went on small walks there all the time, but so early in the morning, they barely crossed a soul. The sea accompanied them at their right, protected by the mountains on their left.

Magdalena allowed the beauty of it all to shower her. Her little huerto at the nunnery was all the nature she was allowed to experience for thirty years. She didn't even have a tiny window in her cell. The outside world wasn't allowed in there, not even through an insignificant square. A warm feeling of nostalgia invaded her when the sea's salty smell came across them. She couldn't be sure, but the scenery was familiar. They might have visited that town when she was little.

"A nun and a sex shop owner." Aurora laughed after the first sip of her café con leche. "You make such a pair."

Magdalena sipped hers and smiled. It was delicious. Proper coffee for once. Aurora ordered some pastries and some pinchos de tortilla for them. The tortilla was just cooked: warm, tender, juicy. The nun's palate rejoiced. Her body warmed. It felt good to be there. Ana's knees were close to hers. Barely touching. Warm. A tingle disturbed Magdalena's lower belly. The adrenaline of having found the cult, the prospect of a satanic ritual, the sweetness of the coffee, the tortilla, Ana's smell...

"Excuse me." Magdalena almost ran to the bathroom.

There was thunder inside her head. Doubts. Fears. What would life look like after tomorrow? Would she be able to... just have a drink with a couple of friends in front of the beach without a single care in the world? Without the piercing eyes of the archangel inspecting her? Not sinning, even with your mind, was easy when you knew the Lord could read your every thought. Would she be allowed to let her mind wander after her mission was fulfilled? If she succeeded... would life carry on until she had to pay her debt after death?

"It *will* be a nice life." The hat man was standing right behind her.

His green, tender eyes looked at her through their reflection on the mirror. They weren't the snake-like ones that he had shown her on the street.

"I might not be a priest, but I'm pretty sure this water is now very holy," she said, cleaning her hands, and murmuring some prayers. "The Lord is with me."

"He doesn't care, my darling."

He hugged Magdalena from behind. She felt his body's warmth against hers. She tensed.

"He's never listened to your prayers..."

"He did answer my prayers back in the well," Magdalena replied.

"Did he now? And did he show you this?" The hat man grabbed Magdalena and forced her to turn and face him.

He kissed her, and as his tongue got inside her mouth, like a warm slimy slug, she was struck by a vision.

Aurora with a white dress, drenched in blood, screaming. A man in a black robe, with a rosary dangling from his hands stabbing her. Her own hands dripping red. Ana, bleeding from the crotch stumbling towards her, two more men in robes following her. Laughing. Magdalena's legs spread open, her vagina tearing. Pain. So much pain. The musky smell of a priest's robe. The raspy feeling of a beard against her cheeks and neck. Ana looking at her from the floor, whispering she was sorry. A dagger piercing her heart and life leaving her.

When she opened her eyes, the hat man was gone. Her jeans and t-shirt were covered in blood, the spear's stigmata opened in her ribcage.

Darkness devoured Magdalena.

When Magdalena regained consciousness, Aurora was applying pressure on her wound, while Ana stood on the bathroom door. The images in her head were still as clear as real memories. Engraved as the two futures the archangel had shown her when she was just a kid. Tears came to her eyes picturing Ana hurt, pleading for her life.

"Ay, monjita, you have to keep your blood inside your skin until tonight."

Aurora's remark made Magdalena laugh. Her touch was like a warm blanket, comforting, healing. The fortune teller placed her free hand on Magdalena's chest. Over her heart. Closed her eyes and inhaled deeply. Her fears. Her doubts. Her pain. All gone.

"You've seen something," she whispered, still with her eyes closed.

"Nothing," Magdalena replied pushing Aurora's hand aside and straightening up.

She couldn't allow that woman to know about the hat man. Magdalena wasn't sure who he was yet. A demon, yes, but which one? His earthly taste still lingered. Had that been her first kiss? It couldn't be because that foul creature hadn't really been there. Was he trying to ruin her cleanness? Trying to scare her so she would run away?

"Is your friend okay?" the barman asked.

"Yeah, she had a... surgery, recently; it's nothing, we'll go home now," Ana said, paying the man.

The three of them walked back to Aurora's place. The one good thing about her stigmata, other than being a confirmation that the Lord existed and that she wasn't just mentally ill, was that wounds healed as fast as they opened, and they didn't hurt for long. So, even before they arrived, she was feeling much better. Aurora walked faster to get everything ready, leaving Ana and Magdalena to enjoy the walk back alone.

"You know I have to ask, right?" Magdalena said. "It's obvious they are going to use your daughter against us... So... I think I should know what happened to her."

"I wouldn't know where to start..." Ana said.

"Try."

ANA

2018

"**S**he has to go," the lawyer said plainly. "I'm sorry, but right now, there's nothing we can do against the court order. We'll fight them, but now, she must go."

Ana grabbed her sister's hand and let out a moan. She then took a deep breath to try to calm down. But it wasn't enough. It took three tries to steady her breathing.

"Clean your tears," María said, handing her a handkerchief. "If she sees you crying, it will be worse."

Ana nodded and wiped her face. Her eyes were red and swollen. She stood up and, followed by María, they walked into Amaya's room.

"Nena, you do have to go," Ana said, leaning on the door, surprised her voice didn't break.

Amaya, playing on the floor with their cat, froze.

"NO!" she shouted, grabbing the cat and holding it to her chest. "You promised!"

Ana's knees went weak. She had promised, and she had reasons to promise. She wanted to go hug her child, take her away, and disappear, but she knew she couldn't do that. They still had a long fight before them, but strength was running low. María caressed her sister's back, and when Ana looked at her, she said:

"I got it, don't worry," and she then approached her nephew.

"Bicho, we all know it's hard, and if there was something we could do about it, you'd never leave, but..."

"SHE PROMISED!" the girl screamed, scaring the cat, who tried to bite her.

She let go of the pet and ran to hide under her bed, crying loudly. Ana's heart broke, and she went back to the kitchen.

"Are you sure there's nothing we can do?" she asked their lawyer, a family friend who tried his best to keep the girl away from her father.

"I'm sorry, Ana; if we don't go down now, cops will come get her. And that'd be way worse for her." His voice left no room for bargaining.

Before Ana left the kitchen, María appeared on the door, holding Amaya against her chest.

"We are ready," she said; although the girl was still crying, she was not resisting.

"Come here, love," Ana told the girl, and she went from her aunt's arms to her mother's while María went back to the room to get the girl's backpack.

"Please, don't make me," Amaya whispered between sobs in her mother's ears, and María had to hold Ana so she didn't fall down the stairs.

"I wish I could, baby girl; you have to be strong for Mama, and we'll see each other on Monday. You'll see: time will fly." She had to be strong for her child.

Amaya didn't respond.

Downstairs, Antonio was waiting, leaning against his car with a couple of police officers standing by his side.

Amaya turned around in her mother's lap to avoid looking at the waiting trio, and Ana could feel her little body trembling when she held on tighter to her mother and repeated, in a softer voice: "Don't make me."

"Come on, I was supposed to leave an hour ago," Antonio yelled from the car.

María gave him a deathly stare while giving him the backpack. He didn't even say anything to her and just threw the pink backpack inside the car recklessly.

"Careful, asshole," María said.

"Ma'am, I'm going to have to ask you to be civil," the policewoman said and earned an even deathlier look from María.

Ana tried to get Amaya to let go of her, to leave her on the floor, but she held on tighter.

"Come on, baby girl; I love you, and time will fly." Ana smiled, and the girl gave in.

She stood on the floor, looked at her mother. Ana could tell that wasn't a loving look but a betrayed one. And her heart broke again, wondering if her daughter would understand her one day; the injustice. Would she be able to forgive her for not being strong enough to run away with her? She walked past her father and the police officers straight into the car, where she set herself on the kid's chair and didn't look back to her mother.

"Was it that difficult?" Antonio said with a smirk.

Then, he took a step towards Ana, but María stood between her sister and her ex-husband.

"Sir," the policewoman warned him.

Antonio laughed.

"Not so long ago, no one would have been able to keep you away from me. You, little whore, couldn't get enough, and look at you now..." He got inside the car and drove away.

Ana turned to María and fainted.

Ana knew something was wrong the very instant the doorbell rang. She didn't want to answer it. Her mother did while she ran downstairs, every bone in her body screaming something was wrong. Terribly wrong. Yet hope, that damned hope, made her run down the stairs. Hope that her child would run to her arms as soon as she opened the door. Ana had never believed in premonitions, and she didn't think that feeling was that: she just knew Antonio all too well... What he was capable of. The lengths he would go in order to hurt her. She had given her heart to someone like him, and now her daughter was paying the price for her actions.

When Ana got downstairs Antonio was standing in front of her with a smile on his face. A grimace. A fucking smirk. He was covered in blood. Head to toe. It was dark, almost black. It was still shiny, wet. She froze. Paralyzed. Ana stood there while he smiled at her. She offered him exactly what he had come for. A long look at her face while he got his last wish. He wanted her to know. He craved watching her face as she came to the realization. He wanted to gorge on that, to see her realize what he had done. He wanted to see her realize her life was over. He wanted to see the light dying in her eyes. Ana couldn't walk towards him, so he walked towards her.

"Remember Llanes. That weekend. I left her in the same bed where we made her." He leaned in to whisper in her ear. "Her screams weren't as loud as yours that night."

Instinctually, as her knees went weak, Ana grabbed his arms to avoid falling. He took the chance to grab her by the arms and lifted her. He kissed Ana, and she tasted their daughter's blood on him. She kicked his chest. She spat at him. He grabbed her face and forced her to stare at him while tears flowed from her eyes over his hand. He let go of Ana when he was sure her life was over.

And then he looked her in the eyes, put a gun to his chest, and shot. Ana could still taste their daughter's blood on her lips. And yet she didn't scream. She didn't move... Antonio was on the floor on a pool of blood. Coughing. Fucking bastard was such a coward he didn't blow his brains out.

People on the street came inside the house. Her mother ran downstairs. She felt hands on her shoulders and arms. Someone hugged her, even though Ana wouldn't be able to say who it was.

She was petrified, trying to find the will to even close her eyes. Everything became a blur. Sounds were muffled as if underwater. That's how she felt. Like she was sitting in the deep of the Ocean. Freezing. Slowed down. Without air. An immense pressure threatening to crush her. Her daughter's screams filling her mind started as a distant sound. That wasn't her life. That couldn't be their life.

When she finally closed her eyes and collapsed in whoever's arms were holding her, all she could think of were Amaya's last words to her.

Don't make me.

MAGDALENA

Magdalena couldn't say a word. All her years comforting the other nuns, learning about God's love and misericordia, were not enough to help her find a way to make peace with what Ana had just disclosed.

"I like your silence," Ana said. "It's better than fake sympathy. *I feel you*, yeah, like hell you do... No one does. So. Yeah. Silence works for me."

Ana tried to let go of Magdalena's hand, to walk inside Aurora's church. But the nun stopped her, tugging on her hand to make sure Ana faced her.

No words were exchanged. And there was no need for them. They both knew. Ana smiled tenderly and kissed Magdalena's hand.

"Hermanas," Aurora said from the door. "Let's go."

Aurora led them from her church to one of the abandoned houses. One that wasn't surrounded by a fence or barbed wire. Once, it must have been a beautiful red house. Magdalena imagined how many laughs those walls had contemplated. How many family dinners. Orgasms. Tears. Only to be reduced to silence.

Abandonment. Ruin. Aurora leaned on the door, and it opened with a creak. It smelled of dampness. Aurora lit some candles inside. There was a pentagram in the middle of the floor. It wasn't the first time she had tried this. Had it ever worked? Had Aurora sold her soul already? Was she eager to get her hands on Magdalena's blood to get her soul back?

"We all need to step inside the circle," Aurora said as she kept lighting candles around it on the floor. "And don't cross the line, despite what you might see."

"I thought you were on his side," Ana told her.

"Have you ever heard the crush of a snail's shell under your feet? Because you step on it unwillingly?" Ana nodded. "Well, we are nothing but snails and ants to Him."

"Yeah, right," Ana replied. "I feel much safer now..."

When all three were inside the circle, Magdalena sighed and put her hand forward. Aurora's eyes shone. She took Magdalena's hand in hers so tenderly.

"Let's see if you are the real deal," she said putting the knife to the nun's skin.

The cold blade made Magdalena's lower back tingle. Ana was looking at her feet. A sharp pain surprised Magdalena when Aurora finally pressed enough to break the skin. Blood came to the surface. It looked as if the knife was a red pen drawing from her hand.

Then, Aurora placed a calix under Magdalena's bleeding hand.

"Just a couple of drops should be enough," she said. Then she poured some dried shrooms, herbs and red wine into the calix. "This would help open our minds."

Then, she took a sip and offered the cup to the other two women. Ana was hesitant.

"Come on, don't be afraid; he would help you heal," she said, putting her hand on the bottom of the calix and helping it up to Ana's mouth.

Ana's eyes were glued to Magdalena. What was she thinking?

Then it was Magdalena's turn. She was terrified. This was the beginning of it all. El Diablo could see her intentions and kill all of them right there. But the

Lord was on her side. The thought gave her strength, and she drank what was left of her own blood from the calix.

Aurora placed a piece of paper onto Magdalena's wound, used the knife to cut her own finger, and let a blood drop fall into it.

"Master, Satan, you are my only Lord, and I will serve you as long as I may live. My body is yours. My life is yours. My soul is yours," Aurora read.

She placed the piece of paper next to a flame and let it catch fire.

"Now we wait," Aurora said.

Magdalena's heart shrank a bit with every minute passing without anything happening. Could she be mistaken? Was she wrong all along?

"Nothing..." Ana murmured.

Disappointment couldn't be concealed in her voice.

The clock kept ticking. They three women let over half an hour pass without so much as blinking.

"Well..." Aurora started to say in a reprimanding voice. "I don't know if you are trying to fool me or if you fooled yourself, thinking you had never sinned, but..."

"Oh, god," Ana whispered when a cold wind blew inside the house, putting out the candles carrying a strong smell of rotten eggs.

A huge black ram peeked at the door. Ana grabbed Magdalena's arm. Aurora smiled, but she was clearly shivering too. She might be one of the initiates, but looking El Diablo in the eye was something completely different. Even the hat man was less intimidating. Magdalena couldn't tell if her heart beat too fast to tell the beats apart or if it had completely stopped. Ana's hand pressure started to hurt.

"I'm sorry," Ana murmured at her back, almost in tears.

"Don't be afraid. He won't hurt us," Magdalena said. "He needs us."

"My Lord..." Aurora was going to walk out of the circle, but Magdalena stopped her.

The ram walked into the room. The echoes of his hoofs were as loud as a drum. An immense heat, like the hot flushes of perimenopause, took hold of her body. Sweat drops fell to the floor, and her hair stuck to her forehead. Her sex throbbed and ached. She'd never felt before that urgent need for penetration. Magdalena took a step forward, leaving the circle. The ram walked towards her. Then its hoofs were hands, and suddenly it turned into a huge man with a ram's head standing in front of her. Way taller than her. He grabbed her hand and licked the open wound with his big red tongue. It was raspy as a cat's. Her knees went weak. Magdalena let out a moan and would have fallen to the ground if the ram hadn't held her. He lifted her and she looked directly into one of his animal eyes. She saw herself. At the bottom of the well. Saw her cousins. Dancing around the opening. Throwing flowers over her dying body. Magdalena's heart broke.

"Al pasar la barca," the childish voices sang all around them.

The ram held her by the chin to lift her head. His hands were soft as silk. Verónica cried through Magdalena's eyes. The ram licked her tears with his raspy tongue.

She started crying harder, kneeling on the floor. Memories flooded her mind. The thirst. The pain. Her tongue, stiff, trying to ask for help. Her eyes barely able to open. Her legs wouldn't answer her. And her cousins singing. Making fake funerals for her. Throwing daisies over her almost dead body. Singing in mocking voices her favorite of Nana's songs. She remembered the tears running down her face when they climbed down to cover her with dirt and make her disappear forever. The firefighters voice. *What are you kids doing down there?* A second of doubting. *She's here. We found her.* Better to be heroes than get caught.

The ram lost his manly shape and left the room in all fours again, leaving Ana and Aurora holding each other and Magdalena broken on the floor.

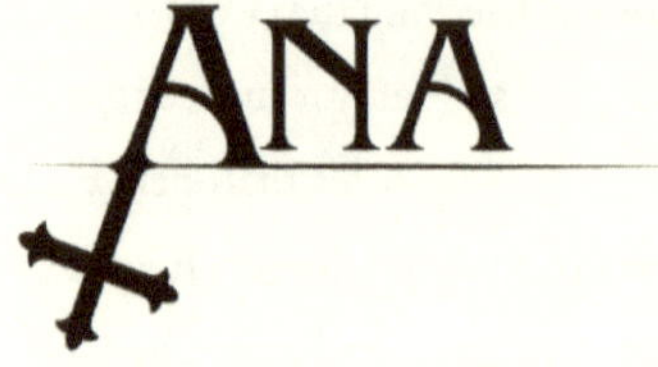

ANA

Ana sat in silence in the made-up kitchen in Aurora's church.

The Ram had spoken to her.

It showed her how close peace was. If she had to explain it to anyone, it would have been impossible. How would she describe the two images going on at the same time in her mind? The strong thunderous voice inside her head while the Ram was at the same time licking the wound in the nun's hand?

"There could be a future for you," he said. "Silence. Peace."

It wasn't the words. It was the feeling it insulated inside her.

"There was just one responsible. Just one. God, who allowed it. In our world, no such thing would ever happen," El Diablo said to her.

And it had soothed her soul for the first time since her daughter was killed in cold blood. Her skin didn't itch. She didn't have that screaming inside her head. There was silence for the first time.

So maybe. Maybe. The end of the world wasn't so bad after all.

MAGDALENA

Aurora sat on the steps of her church, smoking, as was her usual, when Magdalena found the strength to walk again and came out, putting a piece of cloth around the wound in her palm.

"You are the one we were looking for, the Immaculate that was promised, the woman that would set the world free," Aurora said, and it made Magdalena let out a sad chuckle.

She couldn't help it. Of course, she was, just not in the way Aurora thought. The woman was so kind, it was difficult to believe she was a cultist willing to bring on the end of the world. Magdalena would pray for her, after everything was said and done. After the ceremony, she would be free from her contract with the Devil, and she could start over. She would make Aurora understand her mistake.

"How did you join? Why?" Magdalena was so curious the words spoke themselves.

"Well, the whole *it was Eve's fault* never sat right with me, to begin with, not even in Sunday school." Aurora laughed. "I believe knowing the difference between *good* and *evil* is actually a good thing, don't you? Not really much choice but to be on the dark side when you've seen what the church is capable of in the name of God. I didn't have a calling; I had to suffer to get here. But I'm so glad I did."

"Sometimes I wish I hadn't had my calling..."

Magdalena admitted to herself for the first time. Aurora's presence was so calming and reassuring, it was easy to let herself go. The Ram had broken something inside her. She was still determined, but she didn't find joy in her mission anymore.

"That's how you knew we were looking for you?" Aurora said.

Magdalena nodded.

"El Diablo himself told me," she lied. "When I was eight years old, and my cousins tried to kill me."

"Poor thing," Aurora replied with tears in her eyes, holding Magdalena tight with one arm and putting the cigarette out with her other hand. "I'll take you to the ceremony tonight. And we'll make sure, from tomorrow on, there's no more pain. No more assholes ruining everyone's lives. The enlightenment, at last. Go get some rest; you'd need it tonight."

Magdalena went back inside and found Ana on her knees, with her hands clasped together in prayer. Her eyes covered in tears. She kneeled beside her. She knew exactly how a calling felt, and it was devastating. She hugged the woman and felt the power growing inside them both.

Magdalena and Ana drove back to Ana's place in complete silence. None of them ready to talk. Watching the Devil and having him talk to you didn't make for car small talk. Magdalena saw the archangel when she was a little girl; she felt the love of God every day for most of her life, so she wasn't as shocked, but she couldn't help but wonder about Ana. It was way too much to dump over someone you had just met. Even if she had been chosen by God. God wasn't fair most of the time...

"Are you okay?" Magdalena asked as soon as they had parked.

"Yeah... No... Are we in danger?" she asked. "Like... right now? Is it safe to go to my place?"

"They need me to complete their ritual tonight, so... Yes, I think so. My side aren't going to do anything, I don't think anyone knows about what's about to go down. Unless he..." She pointed to the sky, "... had tipped anyone else off. For my understanding, the Lord's work is a lonely thing to endure. No one will know that we have saved them from the end of the world either."

"I see..." Ana replied, pensive.

Storm clouds cried over Vetusta. The whole city was engulfed in a golden storm light, as if on fire.

"But Ana, I must warn you, we... We *will* be, once I have killed the bab... the spawn, they will be mad. We might not survive. I'm sorry I dragged you into this; you can leave now..."

"No, this. I need to do this, and if I die, I die, you know? Everything happens for a reason."

Ana took Magdalena's hand and kissed it. Magdalena retrieved her hand as a tingling sensation pinged on her lower back. The raspy kiss of the Devil in her hand had lit a fire inside her. She could feel it growing inside of her. Making her *want*.

"Let's go order some new takeout to try, shall we?" She rubbed her hand on her jeans.

 ANA

Magdalena wasn't so sure about *raw fish*, but Ana managed to convince her to give it a try. She insisted that the nun couldn't die without having had that experience.

"I'll take a shower while we wait," she said, smelling her clothes and making a disgusted gesture.

Magdalena nodded. Ana took some comfortable clothes from the wardrobe. She left them on the sink, turned on the hot tap, and stepped into the shower. Warm water felt so good. Her scarred skin breathed, relieved. The bathroom lights flickered. The water turned boiling hot, and she had to turn it off. The whole bathroom was engulfed in a thick mist. It couldn't be just because of the shower. A shadow moved in it. Before she could shout or protest, a long, soft finger touched her lips.

"Shhh," the redheaded man said.

He grabbed Ana by the waist and moved her closer to him. Her wet body soaked his clothes. The waistcoat and the black skinny jeans.

"It can't be... You can't be..." Ana murmured, trying to hold to the last threads of her sanity.

"Can't I?" he asked, and the whole bathroom caught fire.

Flames surrounded them, but Ana didn't feel like burning. With his touch, he lit her. Purple flames covered her skin, warm, but not burning.

"You were chosen, just as she was. I can give you your life back. Mend your heart."

Ana started sobbing. She slapped him. She punched him. She wasn't afraid. His presence wasn't terrifying but calming. Someone who would let her unload all her anger on his body. Take the weight off her back. Ana bit his shoulder. His chest. She pressed as hard as she could. Letting all her anger go. Until tears bled from her eyes in cascades that forced her to release her grip.

"I can take it all; no one deserves to carry all that pain by themselves," he said.

Placing his hand over Ana's skin, his stiletto nails, drawing the words, made her scars disappear. He then placed his hand between her legs, caressing her thighs slowly. As he did so, the screams, the constant noise in her brain, stopped. Her heart was light as a feather again, clean and shiny like a loved child's. He turned her around, against the tiles. The coldness of the wall chilled her, it was such a contrast with the burning skin of the redheaded man at her back. Her nipples hurt from hardness. His fingers reached her wet sex.

"I weep for your child. I'll make sure what God allowed is punished."

His fingertips rubbed her clit gently, such a tender touch that Ana couldn't resist a whimper against the cold tiles of the shower. He placed his hand on her mouth and kept going as she felt her body become lighter, and lighter. The scars in her skin dissolved in the running water like they were traced with watercolor.

"*This* is the kingdom to come," he whispered in her ear as all her muscles tensed and the energy of her orgasm unleashed.

MAGDALENA

The road was bumpy as Aurora's car made its way through the woods to their destination. They drove for about an hour before the car stopped. "Here we are," Aurora said.

They parked before an old, semi-abandoned building in the middle of nowhere. Magdalena felt dizzy after the drive. The new food Ana had made her taste was revolting in her already-closed stomach. They stopped before what looked like an old abandoned mine offices compound. A neon sign over the door with pink bright letters covered the gray letters that had once given the place its name. Now, it was just El Agujero.

El Agujero wasn't exactly inviting. Fear struck Magdalena's heart. Her hand was sweaty, warm, and trembling, but Ana held it, hers cold and steady. Firm. Reassuring.

Jesus had doubts too.

Aurora's knuckles against the metallic door were ominous bells tolling to death.

When the gates of El Agujero opened for them, a big, masked man with a tuxedo greeted them mutely. Aurora murmured something in his ear. His eyes smiled behind the mask, and his stare drifted from Aurora to Magdalena. *That look.* The nun wondered how women managed to go about their lives with that stare following them wherever they went. The bouncer nodded and allowed them inside.

The corridor was narrow, its walls rough and gray. Magdalena imagined they must have been white at some point, but dirt, time —was that blood?— took a toll on it, turning it into a mosaic of darkness. Walking between Aurora and Ana, her heart was racing, her forehead dripping cold sweat. A hand reached out to hold hers from behind. The nun turned and Ana smiled at her, holding her hand tight.

"It'll be okay," she whispered.

At the end of the corridor, a tall, tattooed girl who could not have been more than eighteen greeted them with a playful smirk. She guarded a thick velvet curtain. Aurora grabbed the girl's face and kissed her on the mouth while patting her ass. The girl had closed her eyes when Aurora approached her, but she opened them and looked to Magdalena straight in the eyes while Aurora's tongue and hers played. The nun's back tensed. Instinctively, she pressed Ana's hand harder. When they separated, Aurora said:

"Give her your jackets."

They gave everything to the tall girl with *El Diablo es mi pastor* tattooed on her chest and walked through the purple velvet curtains of El Agujero, holding hands, following Aurora.

Aparta de mi este cáliz.

Magdalena's expectations were not only met but exceeded. Reddish upholstery and mirrors covered the walls, reflecting dozens of corners and columns, making it impossible to assess at first glance how big the room really was. Wherever she looked, exposed flesh met her eyes. Feathers. Leather. Silk. Chains. Lace. Lips.

Breasts. Holes. Cocks. Tongues. A colorful palette of shapes and acts mingled as one big moving picture carving Magdalena's brain. Like waves dancing over an ocean of flesh.

Everyone looked at Magdalena like castaways contemplating a piece of greasy meat.

"They are all so eager to meet you," Aurora said proudly with a smile. "And thankful."

Magdalena stopped abruptly, pulling Ana's hand. Ana looked back at Magdalena and walked around her, wanting to protect her. Aurora noticed the absence behind her, stopped, and walked behind the two women. Hugging them from behind, she rested her chin on Magdalena's shoulder and whispered:

"Bienvenidas al Infierno, hermanas."

ANA

A na had been to such places before, but never had she been the center of attention as they were in that moment. Her life was turning upside down. She had seen so many things in the last two days.

What if she was only seeing what she wanted to see?

It happens all the time to people who just want a little reassurance. Grieving, devastated parents that fell prey to charlatans and con artists, just because they provided a single drop of hope. *The clear triangle of unscarred skin on her back.* People would do the craziest things for a taste of faith. Was she being brainwashed into believing? That man, the redhead: he had been there every time. She smelled his breath, felt the unnatural warmth of his skin, the light in his eyes... Was he even real? The cigarette had been. And the fingermarks on her arm. The orgasm in the shower. And Magdalena's wrists pierced then healed in... what? Hours? Minutes? The ram at Aurora's... In the eye of the storm, confused, she doubted her sanity.

And yet.

What if?

Maybe she could find peace again. *Even love?* How sweet were the ram's words reverberating inside her skull. An antidote to the poison blackening her heart. But there was no time to dive into the words or her doubts when a big Persian carpet was removed from the center of the club, revealing a huge, inverted pentagram.

Every pair of eyes drew their attention to them. Ana looked at Magdalena, shivering, covered in goosebumps, and couldn't help but doubt if this was a good idea at all. Aurora nodded at them, moving her head to let them know the nun was supposed to stay in the center of it. Ana, still holding Magdalena's hand, led her to the center of the club. Strange hands reached out with the intention of removing Magdalena's clothing. Men in black robes pulled at the clothes of the nun, who tried desperately to make them stop. Ana saw the terror in Magdalena's eyes. Had she ever been naked in front of *anyone* before?

"Hey, stop, you're scaring her, don't you see that, brutes! You want her virgin blood spoiled by fear?" Aurora yelled from outside the pentagram.

The cultists looked up at the fortune teller, took a step back, and folded their arms.

"Ana, darling, would you?"

Ana nodded. The cultists, a mixture of all that humanity had to offer, dressed in black-tie clothes, naked, or covered in robes, stayed behind. Just looking at Ana and Magdalena. Anxious. Thirsty.

Standing right in front of the nun, Ana could tell that Magdalena was holding back tears.

"May I?" Ana asked her in the most tender voice she could muster.

The room was warm. Silent. Magdalena looked around, but Ana grabbed her by the chin and forced her to look back at her.

"Just look at me. Picture you and me alone. There's no one else here," she reassured the nun.

Magdalena nodded, letting out a sob. Two big tears streamed down her rosy cheeks. Her face suddenly reminded Ana of the pasos de Semana Santa she had seen in Granada. Those suffering wooden Virgin Marys, crying big fat glossy tears.

Her heart fluttered.

"No tears," she whispered drying the wet trails on the nun's face with her palms.

She then removed Magdalena's t-shirt slowly. The nun's body trembled when Ana's knuckles caressed her stomach. Her bra was so outdated, not even Ana's grandma had used those.

"I see the convent is not very up to date with lingerie," Ana muttered with a soft smile to break the tension.

The comment provoked a soft chuckle and a sniff.

"But even in that, you look ravishing," she found herself whispering in the nun's ear so no one else could hear.

When she let the t-shirt fall to the floor, the nun covered her bra with her arms, leaving the rest of her body unprotected. Ana unbuttoned Magdalena's jeans. One button at a time, very gently, as if they were truly alone and she wanted to savor every second of anticipation. Desire building up in her lower belly. She couldn't bear looking at the nun in the eyes while doing it for fear of combusting into flames, as she had done in the shower with the redheaded man. Ana kneeled in front of the nun. She grabbed the jeans and slid them down. Magdalena put a hand on her shoulder to balance herself while helping her take the jeans off. When the nun's legs were free from the trousers, Ana caressed the back of her knees with her fingertips. *So soft and warm.*

"Now for the hard part," Ana said.

She stood again and put her hands around Magdalena's body to unclasp her bra. The nun tried to protect her nakedness with her hands, but Ana held her arms and opened them. Outstretched, like Jesus Christ on the cross.

Magdalena looked so vulnerable in her self-sacrifice. Ana had never wanted to kiss someone so badly in her entire life. Not even her ex-husband, may he soon rot in Hell. As she threw the bra away, Ana placed her hands on Magdalena's hips and started taking her underwear down. She kissed the nun's knee when the pinkish knickers passed over it. Then, as she stood again, she grabbed Magdalena by the neck, looked her in the eyes, and kissed her.

And the chanting around them began.

MAGDALENA

Sor Magdalena was so preoccupied trying to cover her modesty, so surprised by Ana's kiss, and so scared to finally find herself amid her mission that she didn't notice the naked man standing at her back. Nor the blade in his hands.

Ana's lips were tender and wet. Her tongue warm. She understood the appeal of first kisses right then. The kiss was good, but the seconds between Ana grabbing her neck and closing the distance between their mouths had been a blessing. Pure joy. If only their kiss could last forever. She ached to live in its warmth. In Ana's smell. In the sweetness of her voice. In the immense pain nesting in her heart. Ached to drink her saliva and devour her flesh. Chunk by chunk. Make her a part of herself.

Only when the first cultist nipped her shoulder did she snap out of the intoxicating bubble of desire.

It was more itchy than painful. The first one, at least. The naked man, exhibiting his erect cock proudly, placed a piece of parchment to her wound, cut himself, and rubbed his blood on it. Just like Aurora had done in the morning. Only, this time, the man didn't put the piece of paper to the flames: it caught fire by itself, illuminating his astonished face. The ashes flew away while Magdalena still clung to Ana's body.

Silence fell over the crowd. Then, as the ashes rained over their heads like black snowflakes, a rumor like a wave crashed against her chest, and the chanting began again, mixed with cheering screams. Everyone required a piece of La Inmaculada. To undo their contracts with the Devil. To seal new pacts. To ensure they would not perish in the New Kingdom to come.

Ana took a step back, smiling at her, full of desire, but this look in her eyes was nothing like that of the priest. Of the men at the sex shop. Of the bouncer. Of any man she had encountered. This look didn't disgust her. This one twisted her heart. Cut after cut followed. Blood and fire surrounded them.

If it was the time to let all the sin in, so be it. She would embrace it, for humanity's sake.

"Venid y bebed, porque esta es mi sangre," she murmured, inviting them all to take a piece of her holy blood.

The first few cuts had been more itchy than painful, but as they kept coming, as the cultists were cruel enough to cut over the ones already scabbing, her body protested. She stood with her eyes closed and big tears running down her cheeks. Silent, as she had practiced for years and years, as she was when her cousins showed up at the hospital and apologized and she sank her nails into her wounds. In the convent when cold or hunger tortured her physical form. Just silent.

Magdalena prayed inside her head. She imagined Jesus covering his nakedness with a white bloodstained cloth, bleeding from his wounds, muscles tensed in pain, coming down from his wooden cross. His hair matted with dry blood and sap from his crown of thorns. His chest caved in, unable to hold air, walking towards her, every step over his pierced feet excruciating. She pictured herself kneeling for him, just as she had done every day since she married him in the ceremony that made her officially a nun. But he wouldn't allow her to kneel. No, this time, he would kneel for her. Kneel in the face of her pain, of her suffering. He would kneel and lick the blood of her wounds with a tongue as wet and soft as Ana's.

As she felt her soul falling from grace, she wondered: Would he caress her breasts with his fingertips; would he fill the pressing void between her legs and offer comfort beyond her soul? Magdalena's aching mind couldn't help but drift away as she opened wide the gates of sin to embrace her mission. Would her Lord offer her body all the pleasure she had been denied? He was flesh and blood once. He must have known yearning. The aching throb of desire. He must have known agony was just another name for pleasure. Would he run his fingers along her untouched sex? Put his mouth to her virgin breasts and nurse from them? Take out her sins from them like a snake's venom?

Getting lost in her own thoughts made it easier to endure the pain the cultists were inflicting on her. It made her legs weak.

The last parchment caught fire.

Magdalena's soul had been sold.

The atmosphere of the room, filled with energy, exploded. Ana stood right in front of Magdalena. Close enough to help her if she were to fall. Her presence had been reassuring enough for the nun. When everyone else turned to their celebration, all the strength left her body. Ana took a step forward, fast enough to catch her before she hit the ground.

Ana held Magdalena's body tightly. She was boiling up. Sticky with sweat and drying blood. Her body must have been suddenly light as a feather because Ana carried her without effort. She took her to a quiet corner, a bed with curtains and what seemed like a pantomime of privacy in El Agujero, because once the curtains were drawn, holes in them would allow anyone to see inside.

Ana set down Magdalena's body onto the bed and closed the curtains. The nun's skin was numb. Her head spinning. The first tiny cuts had already turned into itchy scabs. Magdalena let out a sigh of relief when the bed's silk caressed her back, and Ana put a pillow under her head, holding the nun's neck. Her body was completely limp, she had surrendered all her will.

"Magdalena, I... what do you need from me?" Ana asked tentatively.

"Tonight... I need you to call me Verónica," the nun said. "That's my sinner's name... The one my parents gave me. I am not Magdalena between these walls. I don't want to be Magdalena when El Diablo comes for me."

"Well, then. Pleased to meet you, Verónica," Ana said, shaking Magdalena's hand.

The nun laughed weakly. Looking at her savior, diving into the deepest eyes she'd ever seen, the painful truth in Ana's soul was made evident to her.

"You want it too, right? My blood, a piece of my soul?"

Looking away, Ana didn't reply.

"I can see the ache in your eyes, the struggle... Faith was a stranger to you and now, you want to know, you deserve to know... If just for one night."

"Wouldn't you... if you were me? If it had been your daughter? Wouldn't you?" Ana said, ashamed.

"You know it won't be of much help after tomorrow, but tonight, we can allow ourselves to be sinners, to seal pacts," Magdalena said.

"I don't have a knife, or the document..."

"No need for those. That's just a show they put on." Magdalena smiled and raised her wrist up to Ana. "Just bite, and say the words," she commanded.

Ana

Ana hesitated; her own scars tingled. Her heart pounded. Her whole body yearned for it. She had had a taste of silence, of peace, in her bathroom, and she craved more. With all her soul. Even if her daughter didn't come back, just the quietness would be enough.

She would make sure it lasted forever.

Ana took the nun's already-cut wrist, where the stigmata appeared when they first met. The nun's white flesh would be so tender in her mouth. Like lamb. She had only once before drawn blood with a bite. Her husband had a scar from it ever since in his hand. She got a pomegranate ring after the retaliation. She knew it would require a great amount of strength to break the soft skin. Hurting Magdalena wasn't among her desires, but she had to. If she wanted the screams to cease.

Her lips and teeth pressed against the nun's skin, then backed out.

"You sure?" Ana asked one last time.

Magdalena nodded and closed her eyes, bracing for the pain.

"Master, Satan, you are my only Lord, and I will serve you as long as I may live. My body is yours. My life is yours. My soul is yours," Ana said with teary eyes, surprised to remember the words by heart.

Magdalena muffled a scream. No one would have batted an eye at the sound in the middle of El Agujero's rising orgy.

As soon as the metallic taste filled her mouth, Ana looked up. Through the curtain's peepholes, she spotted a familiar pair of eyes. Green like the moss of the river. Fiery like her daughter's. He moved the curtain a bit, just enough for Ana to see him clearly without his waistcoat and black jeans. He was scrawny but at the same time so perfect, so inviting it pained her. He nodded, smiling with his sharpened teeth. Ana opened her bloody mouth, looking back at Magdalena.

"Amen," the nun said.

Magdalena put her fingers inside Ana's blood-stained mouth and retrieved them, covered in her own crimson fluid. She then traced an inverted pentagram on Ana's forehead, who savored the rest of the blood mixed with her saliva and swallowed it.

"You are his. For now," the nun whispered under the moaning of the cultists, the beating of the drums coming out of the speakers.

Magdalena kissed her.

"Love blinds," she murmured then in Ana's ear.

MAGDALENA

Verónica was reclaiming the body Magdalena stole from her all those years ago. This tender feeling in her stomach every time she lost herself in Ana's eyes... how could it be wrong?

Kissing wasn't at all what she had expected. First, she hadn't expected it would be a woman's lips she would be kissing. That possibility had never even crossed her mind. But, then again, her mind had been pretty closed to anything that was human, mundane. She had turned her head to her own flesh and disconnected her soul from her body. Kissing was but a simple act. Something small. Not rebellious at all. How many humans kissed all around the world every single second? A sin, though, outside of God-blessed marriage. All those souls condemned every second. Until they repented, if they ever did.

How could that be?

Magdalena let out a soft moan. Involuntarily. She just couldn't hold it in. It escaped her lips and made Ana smile. Magdalena's body was cold. Her nipples hard. Ana caressed the nun's chest with the back of her hand, unleashing an army of spiders running down her spine. Then her fingers caressed the nun's nipples. She had been touched *there*. Nuns her age had gyno exams too. But the doctor's hands were rough instruments that didn't even awaken a tingle.

Only shame. And disgust. This feeling was different. Like a mother's full breasts yearning for her child's mouth, Magdalena also ached to feel Ana's lips. Almost reading her mind, Ana put her tongue to her chest, while her fingers found their way down to the nun's sex. She was sweet, careful. Every step of the way, her eyes were locked onto those of the nun, ready to stop and retrace her advances if their expression changed in the slightest. Magdalena welcomed Ana's touch as if she had been waiting for it her whole life. Hadn't she been saving herself for this precise moment after all? Wasn't she allowed to, at least, enjoy it?

The redheaded man was *everywhere*. As soon as Ana put her mouth to the nun's wrist, he showed up. *Proud*. He crawled under her skin. Inside her ribcage. He was the musky air they were breathing. The sweat on Magdalena's belly button. The pulsing desire between Ana's legs.

He was *everything*.

Ana's desire for Magdalena's flesh was boiling over. It took all her might to stop biting, to hold back tearing flesh and clawing the nun's skin, to not drink every single drop of her blood. To not break her.

The man appeared over Magdalena's shoulder. Bright eyes smiling. Sharp, inviting teeth Ana could feel as her own.

"You called. You signed. Now ask for it," he said. "And it will be granted."

Ana's blood turned into burning oil. Her heart that she had tried so hard to mend broke loose of all the bandages and the stitches. All the pain, all the hatred, came to her tongue like rivers flow to the open sea.

No, it wasn't just silence she yearned.

It was revenge.

Blood.

Antonio should have died that day on the pavement in front of her house, but he was a coward. Nothing more than a performer. He would have bitten down the gun's barrel if he had really intended to kill himself.

"Let him die an excruciating death; let his soul never find a resting minute until the Sun dies, and make mine stop, stop feeling altogether. I'm done with feeling," Ana murmured.

Then, the redheaded man took her away from Magdalena. Ana tried to resist. At first. Her body ached for the nun's. Her hunger hadn't been satiated. Her taste in her tongue was still too vivid. Crimson droplets of the nun's blood adorned her lips.

"Wait," she cried. "She needs me."

But he didn't stop.

"She's got a bigger mission to accomplish now," he murmured while undressing Ana far from Magdalena.

Naked bodies, sweating skin filled the space between the two women so Ana couldn't see the nun anymore. The redhead sat Ana down on a big pile of silk, cold cushions. She shivered.

"Let me show you what you've paid for with her soul." He grinned as Ana saw the flames of Hell igniting in his pupils.

"Close your eyes, and you shall see," he murmured before going down on her.

Through the ripples of her own pleasure, Ana saw the aging face of the man she once loved. *Like the Moon loves the Sun.* The man who broke her. *Like Hades loves Persephone.* Her daughter's father and murderer. Antonio's face was contorted in a painful grin as he was beaten to death by his cellmates. Tangled with the demon's tongue circling over her clit, Ana felt every punch to Antonio's stomach. Pain and pleasure mixed like the perfect magic brew. Every rib breaking knotted with the redhead's fingers pressing gently on her g-spot. Crushing waves of pleasure mixed with the taste of her ex's blood as his lungs collapsed. The demon's throbbing cock inside of her. The knife penetrating Antonio's chest. The redhead's thrusts, rubbing her clit to the rhythm of Antonio's dying heart.

Not once in her life had Ana experienced such delight in the scorching blend of agony and pleasure. Love and hatred.

For the first time since Amaya was killed, there was silence but for her own moaning.

MAGDALENA

S or Magdalena was more than prepared to be disgusted. Repulsed. What she couldn't have anticipated was that she would relish her own fall from Grace.

Ana kissed Magdalena's neck before starting her way down the nun's chest and belly towards her sex. Magdalena turned her head and spotted a heavily pregnant woman in one of the round beds. On all fours, covered in sweat, she moaned, and arched her back as another woman, on her knees, fingered her. Her bulging belly touched the red silk of the bed. A tiny claw pressed the skin from the inside, leaving red markings on it as if a creature was trying to escape its flesh prison. The woman whined and contorted as the claw dug into her insides, but a man shut her up filling her mouth with his cock.

The Beast's mother.

If only Magdalena could kill her right then... *So close.* She could prevent what was to come. Ana's mouth on her sex didn't allow the nun to think straight. Then, pleasure stopped abruptly as Ana was pulled away from her.

The lights went out, and the moaning and music around her ceased. In the darkness, just like at the bottom of the well, a childish song filled the room. Faint. Distant. Then, a grunt. Hooves on the floor.

Magdalena peeked from the curtain; the room was empty. It couldn't be. A cloud of bright smoke barely illuminated the mouth of a black ram. Radiating a light of its own, a big hairy man's chest under a ram's head walked towards her. Time stopped. The same beast that had showed up at Aurora's calling faced her now. As the archangel promised would happen when she was nothing more than a dying kid.

The Devil's erection throbbed when he stopped over her. Moving its ram's head side to side to take her all in. Magdalena lay on her back, spreading her legs open. She wanted to look at the ceiling, to look away, but there was something hypnotic about the creature who was about to possess her. The ram's human hands, covered in golden rings, grabbed his cock and slapped it against his own belly. Like a drum calling to war. And time resumed around them, filled with the cultists' whines and whimpers.

Magdalena's body was weak after all the cuts that stole her precious immaculate blood, after the shivers Ana's mouth sent down her spine. Her legs were sticky from her fluids and Ana's saliva, from her blood. Sor Magdalena had almost reached the end of her mission, wet, spread open and ready to take El Diablo deep inside of her.

Magdalena finally closed her eyes when he lied on top of her. Dripping sweat on her skin like boiling oil. Like the beeswax from the church candles. His animal breath smelled like earth, like life. When El Diablo rubbed his hard cock against her clit, a wave of unexpected, untamed pleasure filled her belly, and she couldn't help a deep hoarse whimper. El Diablo's complacent laughter over her face made her feel disgusted with herself, but before she had time to move, he pushed his cock deep inside her in one firm thrust. It took Magdalena's nerves a couple of seconds to recognize the pain. To spread it from her legs. He put a hand over her mouth when the menace of a scream showed up on her mouth.

Magdalena opened her eyes as El Diablo moved inside her, grunting with pleasure. Every cultist in the room, surrounding them, was bearing witness of her mating with El Diablo.

She looked around, searching for Ana's eyes unsuccessfully. She was all alone. Suddenly, so many hands she couldn't count them were grabbing her breasts, fondling her thighs. Lifting her up. The cultists took her from under the ram and placed her on the cold floor, over the pentagram. On all fours, she could see El Diablo sitting on a golden throne in front of her, contemplating the scene, drinking from a heavily adorned calix. Laughing. Rejoicing at her fall. His cock throbbed against his belly, covered in her fluids and blood, as they made eye contact.

Magdalena, shivering, drowning in an ocean of every human emotion, abandoned herself to everything her mortal coil demanded. She was a meat puppet in the hands of the Satanists. Fingers, cocks, and toys filled her. She pleasured women with her mouth and hands. She welcomed every bit of flesh, sweat, and fluids as her unholy baptism. Cum ran down her cheeks like lonesome tears. For the first time since she fell down the well, Magdalena felt free. Free of obligations. Of duty. Free to allow herself to open up to her own needs.

She was about to faint from exhaustion when the cultists, satiated, carried her limp body, and sat her straddling El Diablo on its throne. He grabbed her face and licked the cum from her cheeks with its ram's tongue. His fingers dug into her flesh, forcing her to get closer. His cock hardened under her. Instinctually, the nun arched her back and welcomed it inside her. Magdalena embraced the ram. She rested her head against his shoulder and rode him. Her fingers sunken inside his neck's black fur. She caressed his horns that burned at her touch.

Sor Magdalena forgot about her mission. Nothing was as powerful as what her body was capable of. No calling. No future was more perfect than the energy of her orgasm. El Diablo's power ran through her. Inebriated her. His angelic light shone under her skin. Without knowing where or who she was, Magdalena focused on her clit against his belly, on their pulsating sex. On his divine heart beating fast against her chest, until both of them came at once. When his fire filled her, everything turned to darkness.

When Magdalena finally woke up, her body ached like never before. The room was empty. Cold. She had been accepted by El Diablo, and now she was going to be allowed into the ceremony.

Look at you. You should be ashamed. Magdalena's heart ached with regret. *You're weak. You were supposed to suffer through it all. Didn't Jesus weep?*

She had sinned. She wasn't pure anymore. And yet it didn't feel like she had lost anything of real significance.

You should be ashamed of your own thoughts.

Magdalena reached out blindly, trying to find a sheet, a blanket, something, anything, to cover herself with. A piece of cloth, a towel, dangled over her face. It took her a second to focus on the hand and the person offering it.

Aurora, with Ana behind her.

"I thought you might need some new clothes. I hope I guessed the size right," she said in an apologetic voice, handing her a new pair of jeans and a shirt.

Magdalena didn't reach to get the clothes, so Aurora handed them to Ana, who nodded.

"I'll meet you, hermanas, outside to get you back to your car," she said. Then she kneeled and kissed Magdalena on the forehead. "Thanks to you, the world will be so different... So bright." She had tears in her eyes. "Thank you, hermana."

ANA

Magdalena tried to stand, but she needed Ana's help to do so. She accepted the clothes and the towel.

"Could you please... turn around?" the nun hesitated.

Ana contemplated the tiny scabs on Magdalena's skin and knew *exactly* how they felt. Itchy. Slightly painful. The look on the nun's face was unmistakable. The morning-after's regret. That unpleasant feeling of guilt, like a lump in your throat. Dry mouth and shivering soul. She nodded and turned around, expecting that all Magdalena wished was to cover her body, to go back to her old self. To leave Verónica's hunger inside the walls of El Agujero.

To her surprise, instead, she felt Magdalena's hands rolling her shirt up.

"Could you?" she asked, indicating Ana to hold the shirt up. She didn't reply but did as the nun asked. "It's in your backpack, right? The scalpel?"

Ana nodded. Magdalena retrieved the tiny leather bag while Ana sat on the floor, still holding her shirt up. The sound of the zipper sent shivers down her spine. Magdalena's fingers traced the borders of the triangle of clean skin in her back.

"You'd never hear the screams again," Magdalena said.

Her voice was different. Darker. As if she herself had crossed a border. Then, the familiar coldness of the scalpel on her skin didn't feel right. Her heart should be going wild, yet inside her ribcage, nothing moved. No joy. No pain. No relief. No shred of the sparks of love Magdalena ignited the day before.

When she was done, Magdalena kissed Ana's neck. She smiled, confused, hiding her feelings, or lack thereof, from the nun.

THE DAY OF

ANA

Ana filled the bathtub, lit candles, and incense. She ordered pizza and chocolate ice cream. Comfort was all the nun needed that day. Offering junk food and a mirage of romance was the least she could do for Magdalena on the day of her own Apocalypse.

Being kind to the nun was repayment enough for what she was about to do to her. Or not do, to be more precise. Not helping, Ana figured, was good enough as a plan. No one would take peace away from her again. Ana hoped Magdalena would fail all on her own or realize in time the big mistake she was making. *How could she not?* It infuriated her, just the same as watching any other toxic couple in her store. Magdalena wanting to please God, and him just lashing out on her and ignoring her, while all the Devil wanted was to help her make the world better.

"You deserve to rest, and to enjoy some random imaginary Sunday after partying too hard; if this is going to be our last day on Earth, you'll get to experience that at least once," she whispered to Magdalena, who had dozed off on the couch as soon as they arrived at Ana's apartment. "Aurora will call soon."

Magdalena looked around, confused. Then she focused on Ana. Her face brightened. She tried to stand, but it was obvious her whole body ached. Placing a hand under her back, Ana helped her. There was some saliva in the corner of her mouth. Ana cleaned it with her thumb. A gesture she hadn't made since Amaya was killed. For the first time, the thought of her daughter didn't spark any kind of feeling. Magdalena blushed.

"Oh, sorry," she apologized, looking back at a wet stain on the couch.

"It's okay," Ana said. "Your body is exhausted."

She took a long, good look at the nun, at her sweetness. Ana could clearly see why she had been chosen. Of all the other humans, more than anyone else, she was just the perfect lamb for the slaughter. So full of hope. So willing. Sweet, but spicy when she needed to be. Tranquil, and fiery when required. All that's human bottled up for over thirty years. Aged to make the most delicious ambrosia.

"My body sure is complaining..." the nun replied. "I feel a hundred years old."

"Here." Ana handed her a pill and a glass of water. "Have this, it will help."

Silence was not a thing Ana was used to. Even before Amaya's death, even before her daughter was born, her mind had been plagued with thoughts, and fears, and screams, and regrets. They arrived with the first pomegranate and never stopped.

Freedom was silence and it was the Devil's gift.

While Magdalena slept, Ana had thrown in the trashcan all of Antonio's poisonous gifts. Even the wrapped up one. What a simple gesture to set herself free at last. After all those years. Now Antonio and his cruelty, his twisted idea of love, were behind her. Her daughter's death was but a sore memory. A story someone told you that once moved you to tears, but easy to forget. The redheaded man showed her the bright future ahead during the cult's orgy.

Oh, Magdalena, how could you get it so wrong, darling?

"Come." She took Magdalena by the arms and led her into the bathroom.

The nun followed her without even questioning where or why. Blind trust exuding from all her pores. A pang of regret should have stabbed Ana, but the redhead's words, running around her lower belly like squirming maggots, were all she could feel.

"I'll let you enjoy it," she said after showing Magdalena the bathtub covered in foam in the candlelight.

The nun grabbed her hand.

"Stay with me," she murmured almost inaudibly, although her expression was clear enough.

Magdalena was confused, and Ana was the only one she could trust. She didn't have enough life experience to tell apart a pantomime like the one Ana was putting up from real love. Real caring. Magdalena could be almost fifty, but she was just as naïve as a teen in love for the first time. Heart yet to be broken. And yet, knowing that, Ana didn't regret what she was doing.

"Okay, I'll stay," she replied, sensing the black void in her chest, the hole left by the redhead. There was silence, yes, but only because there was nothing left of her heart. At least not of the parts that mattered most.

Numbness, however, was bliss.

MAGDALENA

The warm water of the bath was bliss. She hoped for Ana's pill to work fast, for she needed to regain her strength for the night. They would have to fight. They would have to yield weapons, wouldn't they? A knife at least? Would she have to kill the baby with her bare hands? She'd rather not, especially because that would require more time than she'd have before the cultists realized what was going on. *Knives, most definitely.* Hurting too much was not a requirement of her mission. She could have to be a monster but still show mercy. They would have to be fast. She had had a taste of the strength the cultists would have as an army. They could be capable of as much pain as they were of offering pleasure. They would have to do their deed and run away. Fast. Faster than they've ever run in their lives. Or die.

Die.

Both of them.

Magdalena's heart shrieked.

"I'm sorry," she murmured, with her eyes fixed on her knees as two lonely islands on a sea of foam.

"What for?" Ana, who had sat on the floor next to the bathtub, asked.

"For bringing you into this... It was the Lord who chose you when he gave me the stigmata, but I wish it had been different..."

Tears ran down her cheeks at the thought of dragging Ana to her death.

Magdalena had been strong. She had kept it together, she didn't care if that was to be her last day alive, but that was when it was just *her* mission, when it was only *her* life that was on the line. Ana had suffered enough to be asked to offer another sacrifice. She should be spared, and Magdalena would do her best to ensure Ana lived to see the beautiful world on the other side of the night to come.

"Don't cry." Ana kneeled. "Please, if you hadn't showed up at my door, I wouldn't have known peace ever again in my life."

Magdalena wept. She couldn't help it. Her defenses broke when she reconnected with her body, with her humanity. She understood. For the first time, she really understood the archangel words.

For love blinds.

Love was a powerful thing. *Love* was a weapon of the enemy. *Love* was the only thing that could put her mission in danger, for she would do anything to keep Ana safe; she realized this as Ana stood, undressed, and got inside the tub with her.

Magdalena didn't ask her what she was doing. Didn't try to stop her. She needed Ana to hold her. To feel her naked body against hers in the warmth of the bath.

Ana didn't talk either. She kneeled between Magdalena's knees and leaned over to kiss her. Magdalena's heart fluttered.

"If this is our last day, so be it," Ana murmured between kisses. "Carpe the fucking diem."

ANA

Ana's phone screen lit up in the darkness of her room. Magdalena's head rested on her chest. Love was pouring out of the nun in crashing waves. Ana remembered how to fake love. How to convince someone she was falling head over heels for them. She had performed a thousand times for Antonio, and she still knew the routine. She cared for the nun, but caring was as much as she could feel now. Or rather, more than caring, it was a sense that she wouldn't want Magdalena to die. Ana would *try* to keep her safe. To a degree. Unless she was too stubborn to see. Unless Ana had to fight her. Then, caring wouldn't be enough to stop Ana from helping the Devil bring forward the New Kingdom. A simpler one where children weren't slaughtered. Where humans listened to reason.

The phone rang.

"It's time," the nun said with a tinge of sadness in her voice.

"Yes, it's Aurora; do you want me to answer?"

"No, it's okay," Magdalena replied, getting up naked and answering the phone.

She grabbed Ana's t-shirt and walked out the room. The lights went off. *Weird.* There was nothing to cause that. Ana peeked through the window.

All the lights on the blocks around the big white building were off. Even the Christmas lights had died. The night sky was red and angry.

"So, where do we go?" Ana asked, putting her jeans on when Magdalena came back in.

"Well, right at your doorstep," she said, pointing out of the window to the dove-shaped building.

"What? No way!" Ana looked out of the window again.

She would have known if that was a satanist's lair, wouldn't she? Was she finding that place part of a bigger plan? Coincidences were no part of her belief system anymore.

"It's... poetic, if you think about it," Magdalena said, holding Ana from behind. "Like a twisted declaration of love, just like your pomegranates were."

"How so?"

"It's a dove. You said so yourself. That's a white dove. The Devil's own version of the Holy Spirit. Imitation is the highest form of admiration..."

MAGDALENA

Ana left the flat before Magdalena. Both of them carried knives under their clothes. Ana tried to talk the nun out of it, but she was firm. There was no way they would walk into that ceremony unarmed. The two women helped each other tape the knives in places where they could easily reach them in case of a fight. The knives cut into their scarred skins. Everything needed to be calculated and perfect. Thirty years of her life, the whole of humanity's future, depended on them not making any mistakes.

"I forgot something," the nun said as Ana was already reaching the stairs.

Magdalena rushed back in and let the balcony window open. She leaned out to make sure Ana was right about why she had gotten the place so cheap. Her hand touched the white concrete. She squinted to look through the office window in front of her the floor number. To see inside as best she could to memorize the office she would look for after everything was said and done.

Good.

"What did you forget?" Ana asked.

"A way out," the nun replied giving Ana a kiss on the cheek.

More than ever, she was determined to survive the night.

ANA

Aurora waited for them at the door, protecting herself from the cold with a black robe; a white dress peeked at her neck. She looked royal. Gray hair on the loose, killer black, smoky eyes that didn't try to cover her age but enhanced it. Aurora gave her a knowing look and nodded. Slightly sad? Or disappointed? Ana didn't know the tarot reader enough to be able to tell.

"Sorry, we missed the dress code," Ana said, looking at her own jeans and jacket.

"I figured; here." Aurora handed them a couple of thick robes. "Don't forget to put these on," she said, showing them a couple of black feather masks.

Ana put on the mask and the robe. They would be indistinguishable from the others. Merging in. Magdalena wouldn't be able to tell which one of the cultists should be helping her and which one was failing to do so. It would be even easier than she had anticipated.

"I got you the best seats because of what you did yesterday," Aurora said, smiling gratefully to Magdalena and caressing her cheek.

"Please, don't thank me; I just did what needed to be done." There was regret in Magdalena's voice.

MAGDALENA

The inside of the building wasn't festive at all, not like the evening before at El Agujero had been. It was more solemn. The vital importance of the night was palpable in the air. They walked in through the open door at the front. Water cascaded from the roof through the escalators. Nature, as always, prevailed, and weeds had started to grow over them. A path of thousands of candles piled on top of each other led the way down to the parking lot.

As they made their way down, Magdalena spotted men dressed in religious robes. Priests. Bishops. Cardinals. All wearing their masks too. Their best cloths had been taken out of the closets for the ceremony. *Traitors.*

The parking lot had been turned into something completely different from the mall upstairs. Red cloths hanged from the ceiling covering the walls. The concrete beneath their feet was a tapestry of freshly cut flowers. The scent of wax, incense, and roses took Magdalena back to her convent days. Wooden benches were placed in the same way they would be inside a church, leading a pathway to the altar where, in visible discomfort, the pregnant woman Magdalena saw the night before awaited, naked. Sweating. Moaning. Her hands and feet chained to the altar. Behind her, an empty throne reserved for El Diablo himself waited vacant.

Magdalena and Ana walked towards the altar following Aurora, who in-dicated them to kneel in reverence before the Mother. The woman, crying, nodded at them with pleading eyes. On her bulging belly, the tiny claws of the creature inside her searched for a way out. Would it just reap its mother's womb open to free itself? Every hair on Magdalena's body stood up. Her heart raced. She put her hand under her t-shirt to feel the tip of a knife. It comforted her. No more than three steps separated them from the altar.

Drums echoed inside the parking lot, reverberating and adding to the sacred atmosphere. No one dared say a word. Magdalena tried to hold Ana's hand, but she wasn't paying attention to the nun; her eyes, hiding under a mask, were fixed on the Mother on the altar.

"You made it." The hat man leaned over from the bench behind them. "I knew you would, have you figured out who I am yet?"

A foul demon, and nothing else, Magdalena thought.

"I thought you would have remembered me by now," he said. "Is this shape really so different from the one I chose when we met?"

"What are you talking about?" the nun murmured this time.

"It will come to you…" He smirked, before kissing her neck and disappearing as was his usual.

A piercing scream brought Magdalena back to reality. It didn't come, as she had thought, from the birthing woman on the altar but from the back benches. More voices joined in the yelling. Ana stood up looking to the back of the parking lot. Aurora and Magdalena did the same. Flames illuminated the interior.

The long red cloths caught fire.

And so the end of Magdalena's world unleashed.

ANA

na was the first one to spot the priests at the door. Yes, there were other men in cassocks attending the ceremony, but only those back there looked out of place. Hungry in a different way the cultists were. Outraged. Demanding. Hatred floated around them. Rosaries dangled from their wrists, and they held sticks, swords, spikes, and metal bars.

Ana was the first to spot the priests, but she didn't have time to warn Magdalena or Aurora before the mayhem ensued. The cries of the birthing mother were conquered by those of the cultists at the back rows being slaughtered.

God did have a plan to stop the Apocalypse after all, just not the one Magdalena thought.

Ana was the first to spot the priests and, naively, thought the cultists would be able to overpower them. They were satanists, for fuck's sake: weren't they ready to fight back? When the screaming began and everyone turned to look at the slaughtering priests, there was a pause for a minute. Disbelief. Like watching a car coming in front of you in the driveway. Can't be. And yet, you need to react as fast as you can.

"What are those men doing here?" Magdalena asked.

"Your God's backup plan, I'm afraid," Ana said.

"Your *God*, what do you mean?" Aurora interrupted the two women.

"I'm sorry," Magdalena told Aurora, taking one of the knives out. "I'll stop this."

Aurora's horrified expression didn't move the nun. She tried to grab Magdalena, to stop her from advancing, but the nun elbowed her in the face. Aurora fell to the bench, blood coming down her nose.

"Stop her," Aurora told Ana when Magdalena reached the altar where the pregnant woman squirmed and tried to set herself free from the chains. "She'll ruin everything!"

The cultists fought back, but the priests were better armed and trained. As she looked around, Ana wondered how long they had been training for that very moment. Some of the cultists tried to escape the flames and the blows of the priests, but the doors to the parking lot were shut and guarded, and the men in the cassocks weren't about to let anyone escape that concrete hell.

"Please, forgive me, I'm sorry," Magdalena murmured to the pregnant woman.

"No, no, please, unchain me, please," the woman pleaded, looking at the priests coming towards them.

Magdalena kneeled and prayed next to the altar. Ana held on to her, to push her away. If they didn't leave that very second, they would be nothing more to the priests than any other one of the cultists. They had the looks, after all. Having all her feelings back would be better than being dead.

"Let go; let me go; I have to kill the baby before it's born." The nun tried to kick Ana, but she was stronger and more determined.

"No, you don't! Can't you see you got it all wrong! What's the difference between that hellish landscape the archangel showed you and the real world outside those walls?! Can't you see we are living in Hell already? You got it all twisted, you idiot!"

"No, I didn't, I didn't..."

"It wasn't God who saved you from your little cousin brats..."

"How do you know…?" Magdalena looked perplexed among the frenzy surrounding them.

Big raspy hands held Ana's arms, hurting as if they were going to break. From the corner of her eye, she saw Magdalena kicking in the air as she was also taken away from the altar by another man in a cassock.

Aurora's robe was being removed by another priest, revealing a white dress that was soon covered in crimson blood as he stabbed her in the stomach once and again. Ana tried to fight, to kick the man holding her who was ripping apart her clothes. Fondling her breasts and laughing at how defenseless she was. The knives. She had knives. Ana's hand reached back to grope the priests' hard cock, bulging under his cassock.

"Oh, you Satanic girls can't get enough of it, right?" he murmured, excited.

He loosened his grip just enough for Ana to reach inside her clothes to find the knife. She turned around and jumped on him and stabbed him in the eyes, just as she had always imagined doing with the young men in her shop. His blood splattered and stained her face.

"Ana! Stop!" Magdalena cried.

When Ana looked at her, another priest's boot kicked her in the face. She fell on the floor, feeling the familiar pain of a broken jaw. The intoxicating smell of the flowers in the floor like the ones in her daughter's funeral. Another boot landed on her ribs.

"Let her go! We are on your side!" Magdalena yelled.

From the floor where she was being kicked over and over, Ana saw one of the fighting priests hitting the chained pregnant woman with a metallic bat. He hit, and hit, and hit her stomach, her head, her arms, until her skin gave and broke, and she was reduced to nothing more than an amorphous blob of bloody flesh. Magdalena's screams were louder than any other in the parking lot. Louder than the dying woman chained to the altar. The man put his hands to what had once been the woman's belly and retrieved something reminiscent of a baby.

"No!" Ana screamed. Then something stomped on her head.

MAGDALENA

Everything was wrong. So wrong. Nothing made sense anymore.

Who were those men? It was *her* mission. God had chosen *her*, not *them*. Killing the baby was enough, not that butchery. She would have been cleaner, faster. Pain was not the point, but love. Stopping the Apocalypse had to be an act of kindness. Why should the mother die like that? Why should they crash the baby's skull against the wall like Mother Superior used to do with the kittens in the convent?

The parking lot that smelled of flowers minutes before reeked of blood, of all that's rotten inside a human body. There was so much screaming; the excruciating sound turned into a buzz. How much horror could her brain take in?

Magdalena saw the rosaries dancing on the men's wrists as they swung their weapons around. As they blew skulls. As they pierced bellies. There was Aurora, in a white dress, bleeding. Ana on the floor. Looking at her. Muttering an inaudible "I'm sorry" towards her.

As the vision the hat man showed her in the bathroom of Aurora's town turned into painful reality, Magdalena was thrown to the floor by one of the priests. She recognized the hunger in his eyes.

"You are no man of God," she spat.

"What would you know about God, whore?" he replied, kicking her in the stomach, leaning down to punch her in the face with the rosary entangled between his fingers.

When the pain hit, Magdalena found herself again at the bottom of the well. Just a child dying in the dark surrounded by a lullaby, daisies raining over her. Her heart breaking, tiny sobs asking for help, whispering how sorry she was to her cousins. And a powerful being holding her, healing her. Through the white light of the archangel, Magdalena could then make out the hat man's green eyes, and his crooked smile.

Father, yes, and son. Imitation. The Devil's son.

The priest on top of her pinned her to the ground, trying to unzip her jeans. Magdalena kicked and squirmed, to no avail. The hat man lay next to her, his face on the flowers, looking at her as if they were lying in a field contemplating clouds. The spent lights of the parking lot over them the bluest sky she had ever seen.

"I remember," she whispered through the pain. "I remember you..."

The priest's sweat dripped over her face, his hard cock against her stomach as he fought with her jeans. His smell of aftershave and blood.

"I saved you," the hat man whispered in her ear. "When God didn't want to hear. He never listens... You have knives. You can kill this man and set yourself free. You were little then; you couldn't save yourself from your cousins. You're a grown woman now."

Magdalena reached inside her t-shirt and managed to retrieve a tiny kitchen knife like the one they used in the convent to peel potatoes. She stabbed the priest in the eye with it. He screamed. She reclaimed the knife, taking his whole eye with it. The priest got up enraged, holding his empty bleeding eye socket.

"Hija de puta, maldita hija de puta!" he screamed, stumbling around.

Magdalena stood behind him. Holding him tight, she cut his throat. The rage inside her boiled over. The realization of her true mission taking over her actions. The man fell to his knees. Blood gushing from his open neck. Magdalena pushed him to make him fall face over on the floor, twitching and gasping.

She took his metal bar from the floor.

"Pleasure to make deals with you," the hat man smirked from the floor.

Magdalena, baptized with the priest's blood, her mission to completely fall from grace completed with the deadly sin of murder, walked towards the man in the cassock kicking Ana and hit him square on the back with her metal weapon. He fell to the floor, and before he had time to even turned around, she let the bar fall into his head over and over again until his brains spilled on the floor.

Aurora was so close to them, bleeding. Motionless. Dead? Magdalena didn't have time to figure it out, she had to save Ana.

She was all that mattered.

For love blinds.

Ana was all that mattered.

Magdalena lifted Ana, using all her strength, and walked to the side. Ana limped and rushed all she could. The nun ignored the pain in her body; she was used to it. Used to pretending everything wasn't on fire around her, inside her. Thirty years of disconnecting her soul and body finally being useful.

"We can't leave her there," Ana protested.

But Magdalena didn't even reply. The door to their freedom was behind the flaming crimson cloth. The hat man guarded the door for them.

"Do you *finally* trust me?" he asked.

"I do," Magdalena replied, determined to save Ana.

"Then just walk." He winked at her.

Ana looked at Magdalena in disbelief as they started walking towards the fire. She tried to resist, to go back to Aurora, but Magdalena managed easily to stop her. The fire around them didn't even warm their skins. The flames licked them but didn't burn. The door handle, red by the heat's effect, didn't even register in Magdalena's hand. It opened at her command. The nun closed the door again behind her, barricading it with the metallic bar she had used to kill the priest, knowing they were condemning everyone inside to death.

"Burn in Hell, all of you," she whispered to the door.

The two women went back up to the abandoned mall, where the screams of cultists and priests didn't reach. They kept going up to what had once been offices. The nun left Ana sitting on the staircase as she went on looking for the office she had seen from the balcony. *Perfect*. Magdalena broke the window with a chair and went back for Ana, who looked as if she was a million miles away. But she followed Magdalena into her own balcony. Into her dark green living room. The nun shut the window behind them, unrolled the blinds, and let herself fall to the ground next to Ana. Both covered in men's blood.

Both hurt.

Both broken.

Both alive.

EPILOGUE

"Trust me, it's not that uncommon. I would say it's actually pretty normal. You convince yourselves that you are too old, or that it's never happened before it won't happen now, and boom: Baby." The gynecologist laughed at Ana and Verónica's surprised faces when the baby-shaped blur moved on the screen. "Unprotected sex during peri-menopause is like playing Russian roulette with your last eggs, I'm afraid."

"We've been blessed," Verónica, lying on the gurney, said, kissing Ana's hands.

"And the bloodwork came back perfect, right?" Ana asked at least three times while Verónica cleaned the sticky gel from her belly behind the curtain.

"Yes, everything is alright. No STDs, nothing out of the ordinary. We just need to run some tests now because of Verónica's age, but it all looks promising so far."

They drove back home in silence. *Home* was a funny word to Verónica. She never thought she would have one *again*. It wasn't the flat from which they could still see the abandoned building, but Ana.

Ana was her *home*.

What bond could be stronger than the one they shared after all they went through? After all the secrets they shared? Verónica shed Magdalena's skin, her duties, and her fears. She embraced her love for Ana. Even if she could sense that something was off. Whenever she remembered the night of the birth. Whenever she sent her mind back to the horrible events of that night, she couldn't help the feeling that something wasn't right from that night on with her love. Maybe she blamed her for not saving Aurora? But she was dead already... Wasn't she? However, she had perfected the art of disassociating during her convent years, and she wasn't about to let anything as common as her partner not loving you back as much as you do to ruin her future.

She had known, hadn't she? From the very moment El Diablo laid a hand on her, she had known. Verónica had, at least. Magdalena needed some more denying before letting Verónica take back the wheel. Magdalena had tried so hard to deny Verónica the truth. To stop the truth from being anything more than an intrusive thought trying to stop her from fulfilling her mission.

El diablo es un envidioso.

In all fairness, Magdalena never asked *who* had sent her savior. Never once did she stop to think it hadn't been God. Her cousins' ceremonies around the well, pretending she was already dead, were gone from her brain to protect herself from pain. Their games, conjuring the devil to come take their cousin away. Whatever made your pain go away had to be good... right? Had to be... godly? Now, what's good or evil certainly depends on which side of the line you are on.

God had had forty years of Magdalena's life to stop any of this from happening. He had heard her praying in the convent every day and night for thirty years and remained unmoved. He sent his bloodthirsty pigs after them instead. It was

El Diablo who thought her special enough to carry his child while God didn't even consider her important enough to be spared.

The world as they knew it was about to go to Hell. But the world as they knew it was Hell already for a whole lot of people. In the Kingdom to come, Verónica would be the new King's Mother. She would be the one to have given reason back to humanity. Science. No more pain. No more greed. No more children slaughtered.

No more sins to atone for, Verónica thought as she caressed her belly, looking at Ana driving next to her. She gave her a distant look and a smile. Ana grabbed Magdalena's hand, kissed it, and kept driving.

Yeah, you were right all along: love blinds.

THE END

ACKNOWLEDGEMENTS

None of my books would exist without my parents' support through the years, so thank you, Julia Cecilia and Manuel. Thanks to Juan for his love and faith in my words. He gave me the confidence to start, and he keeps me going.

Thanks to Irma Pérez, David González, Jorge Capote, Iria Baragaño, and Lin Carbajales for being the best writing squad one could ask for, for showing up at my readings and signings even when they have listened to me talk about my books so many times they could answer the questions themselves.

Thanks to L.J. Zapico for his wise words, his patience and his beta reading skills. For reassuring me when the imposter syndrome shows up and for being such an amazing partner in crime during signings.

To Patrick Barb for being the most incredible mentor figure, and the best writing friend to have on the other side of the world.

To A. P. Thayer for always being there to remind me, in English and Spanish, that every win, no matter how small, should be celebrated.

To Lidia López for being my favorite first reader, and to Saúl Montes for all the coffees and the patience listening to me plotting these stories.

To all the authors who took the time to read and blurb this book: Angela Sylvaine, Pedro Iniguez, Lor Gislason, T.T. Madden, Drew Huff, David-Jack Fletcher, Chloe Spencer, and Christi Nogle. You are all beyond awesome.

And finally, a million thanks to Joey Powell, the best editor this crazy book could have asked for, and to Schism Art for bringing my idea for the cover to life.